Ron Koertge is the author of several acclaimed novels for young adults including *The Brimstone Journals, Margaux with an X, Where the Kissing Never Stops* and *Stoner and Spaz,* which won the 2003 PEN Literary Award and was shortlisted for the Nasen & TES Special Education Needs Book Award.

Asked how he came to write *Strays,* Ron says, "At the local city college, my wife works with young men and women who have been in foster care, so it didn't take many stories about them to make me wonder what would happen if I put three unlikely types together. I tend to work on the 'What if' principle anyway. It was a surprise to me, however, when Teddy started talking to animals! Lord knows where that came from."

An avid movie buff, Ron Koertge lives in South Pasadena, California, in the house featured in John Carpenter's film *Halloween*. He lectures in Writing for Children at Vermont College in the USA.

Other books by Ron Koertge

The Arizona Kid
The Brimstone Journals
Margaux with an X
Stoner and Spaz
Where the Kissing Never Stops

STRAYS

RON KOERTGE

WALKER
BOOKS

For some fascinating reading about animal behavior, I recommend Temple Grandin's excellent books, especially Animals in Translation *(Scribner, 2005).*

First published in Great Britain 2008 by Walker Books Ltd
87 Vauxhall Walk, London SE11 5HJ

4 6 8 10 9 7 5 3

This book has been typeset in Palatino.

Printed and bound in Great Britain by Clays Ltd, St Ives plc

British Library Cataloguing in Publication Data:
a catalogue record for this book is
available from the British Library

ISBN 978-1-4063-1612-4

www.walker.co.uk

For Bianca,
who likes to have me around

And for Jan,
who didn't run screaming into the forest
when I showed her the eleventh draft

Thanks to Kevin and Carolyn,
who cast their wise eyes on this

CHAPTER 1

I don't know where I am. The social worker said she doesn't like to drive the freeways, so it's just one twist and turn after another. There was somebody else in the van when she picked me up, but he's huddled all the way in the back. I'm in the middle seat.

When Ms. Ervin finally pulls over, she says, "This is where Mr. and Mrs. Rafter live, boys. Get your stuff."

I've only got a suitcase and a duffel. The other kid tosses two green trash bags out the back.

That's got to be Mr. Rafter peering at us from the porch. My parents owned a pet shop, so I've seen that look before. It's the one that means, *Are you going to pee on the rug and keep me up at night?*

Right behind him is a set of plastic chairs, the kind with slats and arms. Ms. Ervin just points. She's big and frazzled-looking. Gold shoes, jangly jewelry, a chopstick stuck in a lot of red/gold/gray hair. A briefcase with somebody else's initials on it. A purse like a bird's nest with handles.

"Why don't you guys have a seat," she says. "I've got some paperwork to do inside." Then she turns her back to the house and whispers, "I had to beg to get this placement. Don't make me look bad, okay?"

The kid with the trash bags twists the tops tighter. He doesn't look at her. He doesn't look at me.

I like to figure things out: The porch sags, the picnic table needs two shims to keep it even, paint is peeling off the overhang, and that's a five-year-old truck in the driveway. So—money is tight. And it's either take in a couple of strangers or dip into the savings.

That's where we come in.

The other foster kid glances at the screen door and whispers, "That one looks like a hard-ass. What's his name again?"

"Rafter, I think."

He points up. "Like in the ceiling?"

"Or on a river maybe. A long time ago you kind of were what you did. So there was a Mr. Shoemaker and a Mr. Baker and a Mr. Fletcher and—"

"What's a fletcher?"

"Guy who makes arrows."

"No way."

I nod.

"So you think back in the day this guy made rafts?"

"I don't know. Maybe."

He asks, "What's your last name?"

"O'Connor."

"Does that mean anything?"

"I don't think so."

"Mine's Porter. Sounds like all my people did was carry shit to white folks."

When animals get to know each other, they dance around and sniff and yip a little and just generally see what's up. That's what Porter and I are doing. Pretty soon it'll either be okay or he'll growl and show his teeth.

He takes out a mobile phone and checks for messages. "Where were you before this?"

I point toward the San Gabriel Mountains. "Santa Mira. You?"

"El Serreno. They fed three of us one can of chicken noodle soup a day and spent the rest on malt liquor.

Social Services drops by, and the next thing you know I'm in the van again." He squints and looks at me hard. Harder. "Charles William," he says, "but nobody calls me that. I go by C.W." Then he holds out one fist.

I know what he wants to do, but what if I put mine out there, then he pulls his back and laughs? It wouldn't be the first time something like that happened to me.

I say, "Ted," and offer to shake hands instead.

He shrugs and does it. "You're cold," he says. When I look at him, he adds, "Temperature-wise, I mean."

"My whole family is cold." It gives me the creeps when I say that because it's a lot truer than he knows. And I didn't mean it that way. It just slipped out.

He pushes past me and heads for one of the chairs. He's a big kid wearing owlish-looking glasses. He sits down and sighs. He leans forward with both elbows on his knees. He stares at the floor.

I wonder if he's scared, too. There's no way I can flat out ask him, though, so I go back to figuring things out: a purple plastic bucket with one stiff brush, some news paper, and a rag mean that Mr. Rafter's wife is fussy. Wipe your feet. Clean up after yourself. Pack out what you brought in. Don't even leave footprints.

My mother's porch was a mess, not that she could have stayed ahead of the animals, anyway. They were everywhere. Dogs, sure, but cats, too. Wall-to-wall cats sometimes. When they were all up and around, the whole floor looked restless.

They rubbed against everybody (and by *everybody,* all I mean is my parents and me, because we didn't exactly entertain), but they couldn't keep their paws off yours truly. My mother has a picture of me with what must be fifteen of them. All you can see is my head because I am buried in cats.

Mostly people dumped them on our lawn or left them in cardboard boxes at the front door of my parents' pet shop—Doggie Dog World. None of them would end up at the pound or in some creepy lab on an island. My mother would find homes for them. Or they'd live at our house. Is that why my father had a girlfriend, that skinny woman in San Dimas who bred Chihuahuas?

C.W. looks toward the screen door. "I was in this place once where the lady would tie off and shoot up while her old man made us paint the house. And all the other guys did was beat on me."

I look toward the big white front door. "What other guys?"

"This lady is not cooking for two when she can cook for three or four and make more money. That's how it works, man. Where you been? There's always other guys."

"Are they ever okay?" I ask.

"This is foster care. Nobody's okay." He reaches under his sweatshirt and rubs his stomach. It's not a yum-yum rub, either. Something hurts in there.

A couple of minutes later, we're all in the foyer. Ms. Ervin says good-bye and shakes C.W.'s hand, then mine. Her blue eyes are big and moist. When her mobile phone rings, she turns it off so we'll think we're more important than any phone call.

She pats Mr. Rafter on the arm, then hugs his wife, who's got big, moist eyes, too. From the look of her, she doesn't jog much or work out, but she's still Nike from her sweatshirt to her shoes. She's got a ton of hair that hangs down to her waist in a long braid.

Ms. Ervin hugs C.W., who eats it up, but when she gets to me, I step back.

"I know, sweetheart," she murmurs. "It's hard."

Both the Rafters lead us up the stairs and right into the first bedroom. C.W. opens the closet and looks in, then gets down on his hands and knees and checks under the single bunk bed like he's about to spend five days and six nights in Transylvania. I wonder if he knows something I don't.

He stands up and kicks at his garbage bags with the

toe of one worn-out sneaker. "Is Ted in here with me?" he asks.

Mr. Rafter shakes his head. "Ted's upstairs."

"Been a long time since I had a room by myself."

"The toilet's right across the hall."

"I'll come with you guys, okay? See where Teddy's gonna be."

Mr. Rafter shakes his head. "Give us a minute. Barbara will stay here and show you where to stow your gear."

I follow him. His big Red Wing work shoes make every stair step groan. His boot-cut jeans are new. His white Western shirt with snaps is so starched it's like armor.

He opens a door to the attic, and the hinges creak. One bed is out in the open, covered with a big blue comforter. But I'll bet it's not mine. The other one is shoved back where the ceiling meets the floor—just the kind of place somebody might've chained up a crazy aunt.

Mr. Rafter says, "We gave the single room to the other boy because I don't like to mix black and white. Astin's going to age out just about the time he graduates, so then the whole place will be yours."

"All right."

"Let's get some things straight right now. My wife's a pushover, but I'm not. Your Ms. Ervin thinks mistakes are things to learn from and a way for boys to mature faster. I think they're a one-way ticket out of here."

"I understand." I try to smile up at him.

He cocks his head, narrows his milky blue eyes, and delivers his line. "For what you've been through, you're a little too together. You're not going to go off the rails on me, are you?"

For what you've been through. He means my parents. I'm not getting into that with somebody I just met. So I say, "I don't think so."

Mr. Rafter studies me some more. He's got big, rough hands. My dad slapped me around a couple of times when he was really mad, but if this guy hit me, I'll bet he'd knock me out. Or down, anyway.

"All right. I'll let you get to it." Then he leaves me alone on the set of *The House That Tough Love Built.*

I put my suitcase on the bed and start to unpack. It's a good thing I don't have much, since all I get are two shelves and a cubbyhole instead of a dresser. As far as light goes, my roommate has a brass reading lamp. Mine's a beat-up gooseneck. I try lying down on top of the wool bedspread, which turns out to be as scratchy as it looks.

The roof is almost right in my face. I take a couple of deep breaths.

When I hate where I am, I picture myself in Africa

speaking Swahili or Chokwe or Edo to someone who knows where there's a western lowlands gorilla that's hurt or sick. The more exotic the animal, the more remote or dangerous the terrain, the more likely it is that I'll be there. I don't own a house. I don't even have a car. I live where chance and necessity take me.

I travel on foot like my native guides. I eat what they eat, and I'm never ill. And once we reach the animal in distress, I sleep beside it. I instinctively know what is wrong and how to make it right. My guides, who are by that time my friends, squat by the fire and watch. They know they are witnessing something extraordinary. The stories they have heard about me are true.

I'm back on my feet in this world hanging things in the closet when I hear somebody go into the bathroom across the hall, then the shower comes on. Pretty soon, my roommate wanders in.

With his shirt off like that, he's a walking geometry problem: kite-shaped on top with skinny legs. Wide forehead and pointed chin. Long, crimped hair pulled back in a tight ponytail. He's lean and wolfish. He's got the only dresser, and the top of it is covered with stuff for his hair and his skin. More stuff than my mom ever had.

He drops his gym bag, holds up an electric toothbrush, and says, "Not just clean teeth, but a higher plane of dental awareness." Then he grins like a lottery winner. "How long you guys been here?"

"Just a little while."

"I was working on somebody's piece-of-crap Pontiac. And then I went to the gym."

He sees me glance at the weights on the floor beside his bed.

"Those are for the in-betweens. You can use 'em if you want, but ask, okay? You can pretty much use anything of mine if you ask." The grin morphs into a leer. "Anything except Megan." He grabs a V-neck sweater out of his dresser and pulls it over his head. "You okay? This all a little too much?"

"I guess I'm all right."

"That bow tie with the camo pants is a nice look."

I don't pay much attention to clothes. I could wear a tux to school and I'd still get called Litter Box O'Connor. "It's my dad's."

"Oh, yeah?"

"He thought it made him look approachable."

"Your dad did?"

I nod. "He said a shirt with an open collar doesn't inspire confidence, while a regular tie is too corporate."

"Could be true. What'd he sell?"

"Pets. We had a pet store in Santa Mira."

"Seriously? Like PetSmart?"

Astin squeezes a dab of something onto one hand, then rubs it on his face. My mother didn't even like to take baths. I'd pass the bathroom, and there she was in trousers and an old bra just washing under her arms.

"Smaller. A whole lot smaller."

"Could you compete with those corporate guys?" he asks.

"We do okay."

"And it's *did*."

I just look at him.

"You did okay. Your folks passed, right? It's Teddy, isn't it?"

"Or Ted."

"Teddy, your folks died, right?"

Is this Astin pretending to get things straight, or is he really rubbing it in?

"Ted?"

"Technically, yes."

He laughs sharp and hard. He says, "We just might get along. The guy before you bored me to death."

I guess this is more of the Getting to Know You game. Well, it's a whole lot better than Beat Up the New Kid. So I play along. "What was he like?"

"Mexican kid. In the system forever. And a total queer.

He split for New York the minute he turned eighteen. What was he waiting for—the lousy yard and a half from the state? I'd have fronted him that to get his homo ass out of here."

"Maybe he didn't want the cops after him."

Astin shakes his head. "That never happens to older kids. Little ones, yeah, because of the pervs and all that. But older kids, no. They don't much care, and even if they did, they don't have the manpower."

I want to keep him talking. I didn't like that other conversation. The less I think about my parents the better.

"Who's 'they'?"

"The cops. The system. Social Services. Foster care. Try and imagine Ms. Ervin in her van stopping at every gay bar between here and the East Coast and showing Enrique's picture around." He shakes his head. "No way."

"So I could walk out of here with no problem?"

"Probably. But where are you gonna go? All Ricky talked about was hooking up with some older guy. That's not your scene. At least not in that outfit."

"No, I'm not like that."

"What you got here is three hots and a cot. Medical and dental when you need it. My advice is hang in there and graduate." He points west. "It's cold out there, man, and when you age out, all you get is a handshake and a kick in the ass."

I look out the little window. "Do I have to ask if I want to go out for a walk or run an errand?"

"Nah. You're not in jail. Just be back by sixteen hundred. Major Rafter goes nuts if you're late."

The light rail system in Pasadena is called the Gold Line mostly to make it different from the Red and Blue Lines, which go off in other directions.

The Lake Avenue station is six blocks north of the Rafters'; my old home is six miles east. Santa Mira is closer to the foothills. It's arty but funky enough to be zoned for horses. The city council voted against a Starbucks. There's a shoemaker and a butcher. And there used to be a pet shop.

Some rich people (who are also green) ride the Gold Line and then talk about the "urban experience." All that means is a homeless guy talking to his hand puppet and a posse of wannabe rappers who huff and puff and call each other "dawg" and "playuh."

The carriage I'm in is almost deserted except for a blind man and his dog—a big, cream-colored Lab. She's lying with her face on her paws, but sits up when I settle across from her.

She looks pretty good. My mother used to organize intervention and rescue because some blind people take out all their troubles on their dogs. But this one doesn't have a mark on her.

I say to her owner, "Since she's not really working right now, do you mind if I pet your dog?"

The blind man turns toward my voice. "I'm sure Brandy wouldn't mind. What do you think, girl?"

Brandy stands up and smiles. I mean that. Her mouth curves up in a grin and her eyes sparkle. I take her head between my hands and lean until my forehead touches hers.

"You're doing okay," she says. "Keep it up."

Now I put my arms around her. I can feel her wide chest against mine, her long face against my ear.

She adds, "I have a toothache."

I pat her, kiss the space between her eyes, then press on her back end so she'll sit.

I tell the blind man thanks.

"Not a problem. She warmed right up to you. Usually she doesn't."

"If you take her to the vet, there's an abscessed tooth in the back on the right. Her right."

The mechanical conductor calls the Santa Mira station and I stand up.

Brandy's owner asks, "How in the world would you know that?"

"I've been around animals all my life."

When I disembark (I like that word. It doesn't sound like forever. I'll pretend I've just disembarked at the Rafters'.), four girls from my old high school pour out of one of the other carriages, so I go and hide behind the big square route map. Only my feet show, and I guess they might know me by my old desert boots except they're not really interested in anybody but themselves. Their sweatshirts say SANTA MIRA. All they need is a zip code, and they could be mailed home from anywhere in the world. And if somebody stuffed them all in a very small mailbox, it'd be okay with me.

I watch them take the switchback stairs all the way to Foothill Boulevard, then head for the outdoor mall and probably the Old Navy store. They've got bags of clothes from the Gap and Banana Republic. But they always want more. Like a boy with spiky hair and a tattoo who'll pull up in a Dodge Magnum, buy them lunch, and text-message a couple of friends. They'll go clubbing and end up making out (some tongue but not much). Then the girls will call each other and squeal.

It all just makes me want to puke. I know one of those girls is Sally Denfield, the same Sally Denfield who stopped me in the hall last year and said, "So, Ted. Do you like to do it doggy style?"

Everyone acted like it was the funniest thing they ever heard. Then they closed in. Usually they just kind of pecked at me until I ran away. But this time Scott McIntyre hit me from behind and I went down. My books, and there were a lot of them, slid for what seemed like forever.

A lot of people saw it and nobody said anything. As usual. Even Mr. White, a teacher who was right there when it happened. I told my father (my mother would have just said, "No animals were hurt, were they?"), he called the school, and a secretary told him the office was aware that a good-natured stunt had backfired and it was being looked into.

No wonder I wanted to go to another school where nobody knew me. Then I wouldn't be candy-ass Ted O'Connor who smelled like a pet shop. I begged my parents to move. They didn't laugh at me exactly, maybe because neither of them had been popular. But they couldn't move the shop and start over, and they told me so.

Well, now I've got my wish. I'm about to go to another school where nobody knows me.

The walk from the Santa Mira station takes maybe

twenty minutes, twelve if you're running from a bunch of guys in a pickup truck. I go up streets I've been on a hundred times, past lawns I mowed when I was twelve because my dad wanted me to "learn the value of money," and then there it is—1117 Oakwood. With its little front porch and green paint (because green paint was on sale and my father only bought things that were on sale). It made the place look seasick, but that didn't stop the bank from repossessing it.

I stand on the sidewalk and shout, "Get out of my house, get out of my house, get out of my house!"

Because there are new people in it. The curtains are different, there's a big, ugly planter on the porch, and a bicycle lying on its side in the Mexican sage.

"GET OUT OF MY HOUSE, GET OUT OF MY HOUSE, GET OUT OF MY HOUSE."

When I stop to catch my breath, a cat makes his way down the big avocado tree, drops to the ground, and heads right for me.

I don't hunker down and make little kissy noises; cats hate that. They don't mind looking up. They think it makes their necks look long and graceful.

"Don't be stupid," the cat says. "They'll just call the cops."

"Who are you?" I ask.

"I live here now. You know how that is. They move and take me with them. Pets are just baggage."

"Were there others around when you got here?"

"A couple still are. You must be Ted. They asked about you. They said to say they're fine. Not all of them made it, but that's not your fault."

"What happened?"

He licks his paw, then looks at it. "Oh, you know. Coyotes, fast cars, pneumonia. The usual."

"Oh, God."

"Yelling isn't going to bring them back," says the cat. "Go home."

"It's just a foster home."

"Tell me about it."

I pet him a couple of times, and we touch noses. Then I walk back toward the Gold Line. I'm not even worried that my former classmates/tormentors might drive by in their shiny cars and throw Big Gulp cups at me.

I'm too busy remembering those last days. I got the insurance money for the totaled car and used a little of it for a farewell dinner. There were four dogs and ten cats. After they'd eaten as much swordfish and ground steak as they could hold, we had a family meeting. The cute ones decided to try the pound and hope they'd be adopted. The others said they would get along as best they could. A big, old scarred tom with a sense of humor said he thought they might stick together for a while. "Look for the headline," he said. "'Wild Cats Bring Down Mailman.'"

I get back to Pasadena in plenty of time for dinner: a pork chop that tastes like a sandal, applesauce, canned green beans, chocolate pudding.

"We'll post a list of chores tomorrow or the day after," Mr. Rafter says. "And we expect you two to do your part." His wife just keeps pouring more purple Kool-Aid. She's right beside me, giving off heat like a furnace, a lot of it coming from her plunging neckline.

Mr. Rafter uses the edge of his hand like a gavel. *Bang!* Down it comes again. "We're counting on you boys to get along; anybody who doesn't is out of here."

He points at me. "Social Services gave us your paperwork, and I don't like a lot of what I see. Seems like you both need new role models." He glares at C.W. "I'd forget about Stoop Dog or whatever his damn name is and look closer to home. Astin here learned to keep his nose clean and he doesn't give us grief anymore." He glances to his left. "Isn't that right, Astin?"

"Yes, sir."

Mr. Rafter lets both hands rest on his stomach the same way some pregnant women do. He waits until his wife has picked up our plates. "And one more thing—I don't want to hear your bellyaching. You have a problem, call Ms. Ervin or see your school counselor."

After dinner, Mr. and Mrs. Foster Parent disappear, him out the back door, her down the hall. Astin stands up and starts to stack plates. "I'll take care of this part and put stuff away in the fridge. You guys wash and dry."

The last time I did this was the night before the accident. My mother twisted a dishcloth like she was going to strangle somebody in a James Bond movie and said, "Guess who brought the Saint Bernard back? Diana Bartlett."

My father let the newspaper collapse. "Well, son of a bitch." It was yesterday's edition of the *Los Angeles Times*. He always read day-old papers because they're free, just like day-old bakery goods are cheaper.

"You're not screwing her, too, are you?"

Dad rattled the front page. "We've been through this, Lois. I'm not screwing anybody. Including you."

I hated it when they argued, and they argued a lot.

C.W. nudges me. "Decide, man. Wash or dry?"

I reach for the Rafters' hot water faucet.

"About time," he says.

Astin opens a drawer, rolls up a dish towel, drops back, and lofts it toward C.W.

Scott McIntyre, the big shot who knocked me down in the hall, was a football player. Just not a very good one. I loved to read about how he'd fumbled the ball or thrown interceptions.

C.W. dries cups and glasses, wanders around opening and closing cupboards and drawers, and gets the lay of the land. Then he laughs. "'Stoop Dog.' That fuckin' cracker."

Astin shakes his head. "Don't mess with him, man. It's not worth it. Take it from me."

C.W. puts a glass down. "What happened?"

"Oh, I did stuff like set my bed on fire, and I was always getting in fights. Let's just say Bob convinced me to channel my hostilities. That's my chopper out by the garage. I built that thing from the ground up. Anyway, Bob's a by-the-book guy. Do what he says, and you'll be all right. She's the nutcase."

"Like how?"

"Wait till you meet Little Noodle." Astin's grin is a whole lot like a smirk.

"Who's Little Noodle?"

"You'll see." He teeters on the back legs of his chair, trying to balance. His long arms are out like wings.

I could ask a real bird, "Why are you showing off for a couple of orphans?" And he would tell me the truth, because animals never lie.

I hand C.W. a blue plate as he asks Astin, "That's it? I'll see?"

Astin nods. He likes knowing something we don't.

"How long you been in foster care?" C.W. demands.

"Forever."

"Here?"

"Mostly." Astin stands up. "It's a piece of cake compared to the first couple of places. Wanting to stay here is one of the reasons I shaped up. What about you?"

"Six years, nineteen placements. Do you believe that shit?"

"Whose fault was that?"

"Not me, Officer. I was in church and everybody there saw me."

Astin comes all the way across the kitchen to grab me by the shoulders and shake me. "So Ted here's the newbie. He probably doesn't know about the dungeons."

Now that it's two against one, C.W.'s into it. "Yeah, and the guy with the chain saw."

He's playing along like he's supposed to and I'm smiling like I'm supposed to, but I wish Astin would take his hands off me. For all I know, the two of them are in this together. He'll hold me, and C.W. will do*f*...I don't know what, and I don't want to know.

C.W. checks to see that it's just the three of us. "Couple years ago this lady's boyfriend was taking dirty pictures of this ten-year-old kid liked to be called X-Cess. These folks not like that, are they?"

I run some water and watch the suds float away. I ask, "How come nobody tells their social worker when that stuff happens?"

"Well, this guy said he'd hurt Sophia if X-Cess told. Anyway, it was just pictures. I heard of lots worse."

Astin scrapes crumbs off the table with one hand and catches them in the other. "Pictures are bad enough, man, 'cause what happens after that is the kid is all bent. He starts acting out, and your Sophia doesn't want that kind of trouble, so she calls downtown and sends old X-Cess back like he's something out of a catalog that didn't fit."

I wonder if the word *trouble* was on my paperwork.

Just then Astin's mobile phone goes off.

"Hey, baby," he says, and he melts into a chair. "What are you wearing?"

He is doing this for our benefit, C.W.'s and mine. I wonder why he needs to impress us. A real alpha male wouldn't care.

"Guess what?" he says. Then he looks at C.W. and me.

"There's fresh meat over here. Yeah. Two of 'em." Then he laughs.

Astin has amazing teeth. C.W.'s look okay, but mine are not so good. Once I wanted the sparkling smile and the girl in the convertible so bad that I brushed and flossed until I hurt my gums and had to go to a periodontist. Specialists are expensive, and when it was all over I owed my father two thousand three hundred and eight dollars.

He had a ledger with my name on it. Black and red ink, mostly red. After the funeral, when I was living in the house by myself, one of the last things I did before Ms. Ervin came to get me was to go into the study, get the ledger, and burn it.

About nine o'clock I find my toothbrush and walk across the hall. Wouldn't you know I'd have to share a bathroom? Animals just go anywhere when nature calls.

When I finish and open the door, C.W. is standing there with a towel around his waist. His flip-flops are bright green. With his big, soft stomach and round face, he looks like Buddha on his way to the hot spring.

He says, "I was with Mrs. Rafter when you all were up here before gettin' situated and she didn't say nothin' about no Little Noodle. How about you?"

I shake my head. "Bob just told me the rules."

"This place don't seem too bad to me. Does it seem bad to you?"

"I guess not."

He slips one flip-flop off, then back on again. "School tomorrow, right?"

I just nod.

"Who's your counselor?"

"Skinner."

"Mine's Yue." He can't help but grin. "Not you. Some Chinese dude." This time, he takes off the other flip-flop. He pushes it around with his foot like a kid playing tug-boat. "What grade are you?"

"Ten."

"Me too. We eat lunch together for a while, all right? Last thing I want to do is end up all by myself at the retards' table." He checks his mobile phone for the second time in two minutes. "I don't know nobody. All my friends are in a whole other zip code."

"Okay, I guess."

"What's up with this Astin guy? You think he's big-timin' us?"

"Probably."

He glances down the empty hall, then leans in. "Lots of times the other kids are in on it, you know what

I'm sayin'? They know how it is: maybe right off it's 'We're-so-glad-to-have-you' and then you drop a dish and they smack you upside the head. Or you wake up at midnight and there's somebody standin' by your bed with a candy bar. And they not gonna say 'Watch out' 'cause it happened to them and they want it to happen to you too." He moves a step closer. "We get through tonight, we might be okay. Any kind of weird shit go down, you yell your ass off, all right? And the same for me." He lets me walk away, then says, "Listen, Mrs. Rafter said your folks bought it. That's hard."

I don't turn around. "Yeah, thanks."

Astin went out after dinner, so he'll probably come in late and make noise. He'll want to make sure I know whose room this really is.

I spend about a minute fussing around with the things I brought. All seven of them. As far as anything weird going on in the night, I'm protected by lions now. They've taken over from my mother's dogs and cats, the ones that used to sleep on my bed when there wasn't any room on hers.

Finally I turn out the light. There's this teacher, Mr. Parker, at my old grade school who goes to Japan every summer to meditate. And every fall he comes back and brags about how simple everything is: one pair of sandals, two robes, one towel. Well, now he's got nothing on me.

I sat behind Penny Raybon in Mr. Parker's class. She was the one who had that stupid party where I got in trouble.

We played dumb games until Penny's parents left, then it was time for Seven Minutes of Heaven. Except the girls said I smelled like cat pee, so all I got to do was lead the lucky couples into the bedroom.

While I waited and watched the clock, I wandered around and looked in drawers and closets. They had so much stuff. I grabbed a letter opener and scratched my initials in their desk.

In the principal's office the next day, I said I didn't know why I did it. My mother walked to the window and cooed to some pigeons, and my father said to the Raybons, "I'll pay for the desk and I'll guarantee nothing like this will ever happen again." I'm surprised he didn't give them a discount coupon for a spaniel.

I didn't even get detention, but Penny made sure nobody ever forgot.

The house shifts and creaks a little. I hear somebody on the stairs and the television set laughing at itself.

When Astin opens the door, light cuts across his part of the room. He's still on his mobile phone and acts like he's alone. "I'm sorry, too," he says, "but wasn't it fun making up?" He doesn't even bother to look at me. "For sure," he says. "See you tomorrow. Me too. Yeah."

I hear his boots drop and his shirt fly off. It's like he's undressing over the speed limit.

He walks over to his weights barefoot and does some exercises. He groans a little, huffing and puffing like the wolf in the three little pigs story, then drops his dumbbells on purpose.

"You awake, Teddy?"

"What do you think?"

"You ever work out?" he asks.

"No."

"You should work out."

"I hate athletes."

"It's not so you can play sports. It's so you can get laid."

I sit up in bed. "Oh, please."

"Get up."

"No."

He strides toward my bed. "Don't be a candy ass. C'mon."

Oh, man. Here we go, I'll bet. Just what C.W. said: Beat

Up the New Guy. The funny thing is, I don't much care. I just want to get it over with.

He hands me two shiny dumbbells. He presses my elbows into my sides. "Now curl those up toward your shoulders."

I do it, but I'm thinking I'm pretty close to the door. I could drop these and run.

"Ten times." He steps back and watches. "Good. Feel that?" He takes hold of my biceps.

I nod as I step away.

"This is low weight/high reps. Like eight times a day. Plus some shoulder stuff. And some lat work. You're not gonna bulk up like Arnold. You're gonna get lean and mean. Girls want something hard to hold on to beside your pecker."

Maybe he's not a goon, just a gym teacher. I put the weights down next to the others.

"Good for you, man. That's where they belong. Use 'em whenever you want, but put 'em back. And don't touch anything else. I'm fanatical about my stuff, okay?"

"Okay."

"Stick to the program and in three months you'll see the difference. It takes like thirty minutes a day and then you're not ashamed to look in a mirror anymore." He throws back the bright blue blanket, gets into bed, and turns out the light. His light. "Silk sheets," he says. "You ever sleep on silk sheets?"

"No."

"They don't cost that much. You got any money?"

"Some."

"Good. Let's get you some silk sheets."

So this is foster care—a top sergeant in a cowboy shirt, gallons of purple Kool-Aid, a sinister Noodle, and weight-lifting lessons in the middle of the night.

CHAPTER 2

MY FIRST DAY OF SCHOOL

It was very big.

There were many people.

I talked to a counselor and I met Astin's girlfriend.

Then I went home.

That's the short version. C.W. and I walk there together. It's not far, maybe ten blocks. All the neighborhood dogs come out because it's fun to bark at kids. But when they see me, they stop. I tell them, "It's okay; go on and enjoy yourselves."

Closer to school, the scene is a lot like the one at Santa Mira: a van with a hundred WROQ stickers, somebody trying to patch out in his mother's old Toyota and a VW with Stonehenge-size speakers. The only thing missing is Scott McIntyre in his Mustang with a Slurpee he bought just to throw at me.

One or two kids dribble out of every front door and join up with another dozen. They spill into the street, then rush downhill—a river of hoodies, sneaks, jean jackets, and backpacks.

All around C.W. and me, people shout at each other using the secret code they learned from MTV. "Hey, bay!" "You come through later, okay?"

I didn't talk to my classmates much, mostly grown-ups like my parents and teachers and people who came into the pet shop. I don't think many patrons wanted to hear me say, "Why you buggin', bustah? You know I'm down with yo pooch."

But all the noise does remind me to keep my voice as deep as I can. Not that my voice is high. Not very high, anyway.

C.W. and I make our way to King/Chavez High, Land of the Colored Martyrs. We walk between two murals—Martin Luther King all pained but optimistic, and Cesar Chavez all noble and determined.

"I hate the first day," C.W. says. "You make one mistake and that's it, man. For the rest of your life you're the guy who farted in gym or the poor fuck who fell down goin' up the stairs. Jail is easier. In jail the first thing you do is find some punk, kick his ass, and that's that."

"When were you in jail?"

"I wasn't, but I know guys who were." He looks me up and down. "Why'd you wear those stupid pants? You gonna be the guy in the stupid pants forever, you know that, don't you?"

"These are old, but they're Ralph Lauren cords, okay?"

"Now you're fuckin' gay. Get away from me."

We stand in the quadrangle and turn the map in my orientation packet upside down, then right side up, then upside down again. C.W. hails a couple of guys who are wearing the same Kobe tank top he is, but—believe it or not—bigger. All three of them have on yellow work shoes like the bulldogs who run steam shovels in cartoons.

"Where's the administration building?" C.W. asks.

They fool around with their shades. They look at me, then at each other. One leans north, the other south. Then they stagger off, laughing.

"A hundred brothers to choose from," C.W. says, "and I get a couple of wankstas."

My parents wouldn't know what to make of King/Chavez. It's too much like downtown Los Angeles: graffiti, trash, drug dealers, criminals around every corner. My mother couldn't get over this story about some woman in New York named Kitty who was beaten and raped while people—neighbors, some of them—watched and didn't do anything.

Just then a scuffle breaks out twenty yards away, and nobody pays any attention. At Santa Mira High somebody would have yelled, "Fight! Fight!" Not here.

C.W. points to the kid on the ground. "Maybe he knows where the fuckin' administration building is."

I ask a couple of skateboarders. But young ones, not the really scary kind who stick up 7-Elevens on their way to empty somebody's pool.

They size me up. The one with porcupine hair and an eye inked on his wrist answers, "Bungalow with the A on it about two over from here."

"You transfer in?" asks his friend, who's got music coming out of him from who-knows-where.

I nod.

"Well, don't leave your luggage unattended."

They crack up and roll away, already buzzed on something at seven forty-five in the morning.

I look down at my feet. Sometimes I get this feeling

about the ground I'm standing on. About what it knows. All the things it's seen and been through. And it's still here, anyway.

That always makes me feel a little better. There were horses and wagons once. People worked hard and were nice. If somebody's parents died, the nearest neighbors took him in.

Ms. Ervin said she would fax things over and she did, so we okay some paperwork, fill out some more, and then find the counseling center, which is enormous. Rows and rows of orange chairs—the plastic, easy-to-keep-clean kind for the bleeders and the weepers. Doors all around like some nightmare version of *Let's Make a Deal.* Every now and then, one of the doors opens and a counselor with a manila folder in his or her hand butchers the next name.

C.W. gets called right away: "D.W. Potter?"

I sit down a couple of seats away from a girl with twenty or so piercings in each eyebrow. Silver rings like the kind that hold up shower curtains, but a lot smaller. She's wearing a white long-sleeved top and an all-the-way-down-to-her-ankles blue skirt. It's like her head goes to raves and her body goes to church.

Pretty soon a guy whose blond hair is starting to turn green settles down between us.

"Hey, man," he says.

"Yeah, hi."

He leans in and kind of points with the cast on his broken hand. "You know this girl over here?"

"No, I'm afraid not. I just moved here so—"

"What are you reading?" he asks her, turning his back on me.

She holds up the paperback in her lap.

He scoots closer. "What class is that?"

"It's just for fun."

"Wow. Far out. What're you here for? I gotta clear a few things up. I used my computer to enroll in summer school and got three English classes, one of 'em at midnight."

If I lean back, I can see her smile at him.

"Summer school's a drag," she says.

"Tell me about it. But I got no choice. I was a movie star for a couple of months, so I missed a lot of classes."

She shifts so she's facing him. "You know Tom Cruise?"

"Not exactly. I mean I got paid, so I could help my mom with the rent, and I bought a van and all. But mostly I just partied." He waggles his cast. "Now this and they're like, 'See you, dude.' And I'm like, 'What about my check?' And they're all, 'Read the fine print, man.'"

"Maybe you need an agent."

She's kidding him, but playing along too. How did he get her to do that?

He shakes his head. "I'm glad to be out of it, you know what I mean? Surfing's supposed to be fun, but they were always, 'Show up on time, Derek.' 'Do that again, Derek, and look at the camera.' And I'm like, 'Every time is different, fucker. I can't fucking just do it again. It's the ocean, man. Not a wave factory.' You know what I'm sayin'?"

"So," she asks, "do you have to give the money back?"

"Nothin' to give back, babe. The money's gone."

Out comes her hand. "I'm Angie."

"I'm Derek." He keeps holding her hand. "I've seen you around."

A door opens and I hear, "Mr. O'Collar?"

I tell him, "It's O'Connor."

My counselor, Mr. Skinner, flips through my permanent record, glancing up every now and then to make sure I am still there. Seeing him reminds me of what C.W. and I talked about a couple of days ago—how people used to be named after their jobs.

Mr. Skinner is big but not soft, has a handlebar mustache, and wears cowboy boots. He looks like he could drive a mule team. Or gut a moose and cure the hide.

On the wall behind him stands a rack full of pamphlets featuring Top Ten schools with huge buildings and fascinated students seated in a circle listening to some guy with a beard. There's never anything closer to the truth, which would be a city college campus with hollow-eyed stoners huffing glue out of Burger King bags.

"How are you getting along?" He taps the folder. "You've been through a lot."

"I'm okay, I guess."

"Is there anybody you can talk to?"

"I've got friends," I lie, "if that's what you mean."

"I was thinking more along the lines of a professional."

"My social worker calls me a lot. And comes over all the time."

He strokes his mustache. On the wall by his desk a plaque says VIOLENCE DEGRADES EVERYONE IT TOUCHES.

Really? Scott McIntyre never seemed too degraded after knocking me around. Neither did those guys who put the stink bomb in my locker. Or even the girls who said I smelled like a wet dog and knocked me off the monkey bars.

"And this social worker," he says, "has access to psychologists, grief counselors, that kind of thing?"

I nod.

"Who decides when you should talk to one of those?"

"She does, I guess."

"But you don't feel the need."

"I trust Ms. Ervin. She's, you know, kind of like a mom."

He tries his X-ray vision on me, but I am wearing my impenetrable suit.

"Well, all right. As long as you're talking to somebody."

I know my parents are dead, but going over and over it isn't going to help. The lions in my bedroom help. The giraffe in the backyard really helps. E specially the giraffe—that long, sweet face and those eyelashes.

"We've got peer counseling here, Todd. Did you know that?"

I shake my head, but I do know. In one of the orientation pamphlets there's a picture of the Deeply Furrowed advising a boy with a bowl haircut to stop being such a simpleton.

"If you're interested," he says, "I can set up an appointment."

"Sure."

He writes on a Post-it note, then sticks that onto his computer with about a dozen others.

Mr. Skinner says, "This is a chance for a fresh start, Tom. Take it."

"Yes, sir." Yes, sir. Three bags full.

"All right, then." He heaves himself to his feet and holds out an enormous paw.

That's how I can stand this, by pretending he's a bear. I was at the zoo once on a field trip and one of the bears was singing its death song. The teachers couldn't tear me away from the cage, and I couldn't stop crying.

Imagine what my classmates did with that.

We know where the administration building is, so C.W. and I meet by the steps, then walk toward the cafeteria. We eat at eleven-thirty, part of the first shift.

"You okay?" he asks.

I nod. "I was waiting to see Mr. Skinner, and I heard this surfer tell some girl how he'd blown a whole bunch of money."

"Chicks love that reckless shit, don't they?"

"Don't ask me."

"Anybody give you grief about those pants?"

"You should talk. What size are yours—Double Extra Large Tremendous?"

All of a sudden he grabs me, pulls me close, and whispers, "How long we been here?"

"At school? Since a little before eight."

"Guess how many fools asked if I was holding. Talk about stupid. 'Lookee here. A new jiggah. Let's see if he's got some weed.' I could be a narc. I could be anything. But they just walk up like I'm a fuckin' vending machine and ask for a dime bag. I already got to write a paper for Introduction to Black Studies, and guess what it's gonna be about?"

"Jumping to conclusions?"

"For sure." C.W. slaps at his pockets. "You got a pen?"

I've got everything. And it's well organ ized, too. How pathetic is that? I imagine talking to that girl in the counseling center: "Yeah, I'm totally crazy. I mean, it's the first day of school and I've only got one refill for my gel pen!"

I hand C.W. a new Biro, one of the ones that Mrs. Rafter probably had to buy for us. She passed them out this morning, then stood on the porch and watched us leave. I wonder what she does all day.

C.W. opens the door to the cafeteria. There are already people eating, so I get the whole feedlot atmosphere—the chewing, the lowing, the milling around.

I step out of the way when somebody from the other side of the room bellows, "Yo, C.W.!"

"Listen," he says, "I'm gonna eat with these guys."

"Which guys?"

"Just these guys."

I watch him head for his new friends. He's got his middle and index fingers tucked into his palms, his shoulders roll forward, he's bobbing his head.

If my father saw him come into the store, he'd lock the cash register. I know C.W. dresses tough and talks tough, but I'm not sure he is.

Bored ladies in hairnets wave shiny metal spoons around. The line that leads to a ton of sloppy joes is really long. But there's a lighted box of portable food by the west wall. That's for me.

I take my sandwich outdoors. The indestructible metal tables are wobbly and scratched. A boy with acne so bad his face looks like it needs medical attention talks into a mobile phone: "It can't be downhill salmon, man. A salmon's a fish, and we're talking about skiing."

A girl in a wheelchair types on a laptop with one finger. I have to talk myself into it, but finally I go over and ask, "I'm kind of new here. Mind if I sit with you?"

She just points. "There's room over there."

Shot down again. I should know better. Actually I do know better, but, God, wouldn't you think the pariahs would band together so we could roll and lurch through the halls, terrifying the pretty and the celebrated? It never happens.

I inspect my stupid sandwich: a slice of turkey I can see through, lettuce wilted and brown around the edges, bulletproof cheese. Sparrows land on the edge of the table and say, "Please!" So I feed them pellets of bread.

"Free as a bird" is a dumb thing to say. Gray sparrows like these almost never go farther than a mile from where they're born. They eat, mate, and die.

Which is what my parents did.

A week or so ago, Ms. Ervin told me that I was still in shock and that when what happened really hit me, I should call her. She just wants me to cry my little eyes out.

Animals never cry. They don't go to pieces and call somebody and go through a box of Kleenex an hour. A lot of times they sniff the body, and that's that.

The lions get under the covers with me at night, and when they do, I think about my mother whether I want to or not. She always had four or five dogs on her bed. She wasn't like any other mother I'd ever heard of: no PTA, and fish sticks for Thanksgiving. But everything I know about animals I learned from her.

"Think about something else, Ted," says the nearest sparrow.

The floor of this outdoor patio isn't poured concrete but brick. A gift—says the brass plaque—from the Class of '02. Ants are everywhere, burrowing into the packed dirt and motoring toward their underground home.

I drink my milk, watch them pick up crumbs twice their size, then line up like they're on safari. Which reminds me of Africa. Man, if I was in Africa, everybody would want to sit at my table.

"Ted!"

I look up and see Astin bearing down on me. His arm is around a girl who looks like the source of many a hopeless crush. She's dressed like a musketeer in really tall boots and one of those short jackets with loops and wooden things instead of buttons. Astin whispers something to her, and she slaps at him.

I wonder what he said, or maybe it's just how he said it. I'm terrible around girls, not that I've been around that many. I always say the wrong thing. Or the right thing the wrong way. Or both.

"What's up, my man?" he asks.

His girlfriend waits for me to answer.

I glance away from the ants. That surfer in the counseling center got along with that Angie by telling stories. So I say, "I was just thinking about locust forecasting."

Astin grins at the girl. Except for the purple streak, her hair is the color of old silverware. Then he points back and forth a couple of times. "Megan, Ted. Ted, Megan."

She asks, "What, pray tell, is locust forecasting?"

"It's just a guy with agents in the field, and they call in with data about drought and winds and things like that." I know I'm talking too fast. *Slow down, Teddy.* "All of which goes into a computer and then you know when the locusts will arrive."

"This would be some other place without a Starbucks every two blocks."

"Yes. Africa, mostly."

"And once you know the locusts' estimated time of arrival?"

"Get the Raid," says Astin.

"It's better to know than not. Maybe get the crops in early. Maybe just take the babies and get out of the way."

"And this," Megan asks, "is a real job?"

I nod.

"Didn't some guy in the Bible eat locusts and honey?" Astin asks.

Megan pretends to be stunned. "You never fail to surprise me."

"Mrs. Rafter used to read me stories while she gave me a bath."

"Lucky Mrs. Rafter. And so dexterous."

I tell them, "There's a tree called a locust, which is a kind of carob. So that guy was probably eating honey and chocolate."

Megan nods. "You must be one of the smart ones."

I shrug and say, "And you must be one of the popular ones."

"Oh, sweetie," she protests. "I'm just visible. There are girls in this school who could knock me down and give me a black eye and I'd just be grateful for the attention. And you can tell how divine they are because they are never on the phone. I, on the other hand, could not live without mine."

Hers goes off right on cue. She grins, showing advertisement-quality teeth as she says, "Hi. In the Pit. Sure." Then she tells Astin, "Belle's coming."

"Then we should either get the crops in early or take the babies and get out of the way."

Megan slaps at Astin the way girls do when they're with boys they like.

When her phone rings again, he pretends to be fed up and pushes her out of the way.

"Your classes okay?" he asks me.

"I guess. In English I learned Shakespeare was a playwright."

"Who's your homeroom teacher?"

"Mr. Decker."

"He's cool. How about your counselor?"

"Skinner."

"That jerkwad. He still calls me Tex."

"Because Astin sounds like Austin, which reminds him of Texas."

"Bingo. Where's C.W., anyway?"

"Eating with his new friends."

Astin shakes his head. "I'm telling you, man, drop one of the brothers in the middle of nowhere and before you know it four or five hood rats show up and they make a rap video."

This girl, who must be Belle, glides through the door leading out of the cafeteria. She's pale and thin and dressed in gauze. She kisses Astin on the cheek, and he acts like he's getting a penicillin shot. Then she clings to Megan, who chants, "Belle, Ted."

Belle winds herself around me like this boa constrictor my parents had in the shop for a while. "Oh, my God," she says. "It's the orphan."

CHAPTER 3

It's a Saturday morning. The house is almost empty. Mr. Rafter's truck, a Ford F-150, is gone, and so is Astin's motorcycle. C.W. left right after breakfast to play basketball.

When I'm alone like this and I know Astin's not coming back for a while, there's this thing I do. I put on one of his leather jackets and get out my homework. I pretend I'm somebody else. Not Astin, but not me either.

This boy, whoever he is, isn't president of his class or valedictorian, but he's still smart. He knows a lot of people but only has a few close friends, kids he's known almost all of his life. If somebody has a problem, they call him and talk. He doesn't pick fights, but he never backs down.

Basically he's just a guy who lives in a nice house. He's got an okay car and a girlfriend who doesn't want to go all the way. His parents love each other and take turns cooking dinner.

That's it. When the essay for English is done or I've solved all the algebra problems for Monday, I hang the jacket back up. Then I'm just Ted O'Connor again, who's got an appointment with his social worker.

At twenty after ten, Ms. Ervin shows up in her rattle-trap van. I meet her at the door and we shake hands.

"Do you mind if we talk on the porch, Teddy? It's not cold out and I have to keep an eye on these boys."

I can see both of them with the hoods of their sweat-shirts up. They might be monks on their way to a retreat. But they're not; they're kids that nobody wants.

She sits down in one of the phony Adirondack chairs. Her watery eyes flick from the papers in her lap to the van and back again.

"How are you getting along, Ted?"

"Pretty well, I guess."

"Any problems?"

I feel like she's in my room, going through my things. I just need to get through this and she'll leave me alone. I lean toward her. "I like that blouse. Those are mother-of-pearl buttons."

She asks, "How in the world do you know something like that?"

Her smile is so big and real that I'm kind of sorry I can't do what she wants and start crying big-time. But that would mean I'd have to remember everything all at once.

"Dad hated paying babysitters, so Mom dragged me to thrift stores and yard sales when I was little. My job was checking buttons."

All of a sudden she stands up and shouts, "LeBraun! What do you think you're doing? Take Winston and get back in the van!"

LeBraun says, "We was just gonna play some catch."

"Well, not in the street," Ms. Ervin says. "By the side of the van, where I can see you." Then she returns to me. "I'm sorry, Ted. Where were we?"

"We were talking about my mother."

"Oh, that's right. Do you miss her?" She tries to act casual, but we're in Freudland now. On our left is Sigmund Village, and on our right the Oedipus Complex.

I say, "She drove me crazy sometimes. You know what good clothes are?" I ask.

She nods, glances at the orphans, then back at me. "Sure. Things to wear to dinner out or church. Anything that isn't everyday."

"Right. Well, I had clothes that were supposedly so good I couldn't wear them."

"Never?"

I nod.

"And how did you feel about that?"

Oh, man. Right out of chapter 1: Dealing with the Troubled Child.

"They were used, Ms. Ervin. Somebody else wore them. Why couldn't I?"

"And that made you angry."

"How do you know how I felt about anything?"

"Good, Teddy. Let those emotions boil up. So you had intense, painful feelings. You had them then and you have them now. How do you handle them? Do you cry, do you throw things, do you sleep twelve hours in a row?"

I've got to start some serious lying.

I swallow hard and whisper, "I cry at school sometimes."

That makes her sit up. "Really?"

"Only in Dr. Skinner's office. Not, you know, where people can see me. Just where it's safe."

"And this Dr. Skinner is—?"

"My counselor. He's real accessible, and he likes me a lot."

"So there's someone you can open up to."

I nod. "And Astin, sometimes. And C.W. They're good guys."

"Not the Rafters?"

"Gee, I couldn't cry in front of Mr. Rafter. He'd tell me to drop and give him twenty."

She leans back and laughs. It was the "Gee" that did it. She closes her folder and gets to her feet. "Well, I think we made some real progress here."

Which is exactly what I want her to think. But all the lying just wore me out. What's the point of telling anybody how you really feel, anyway? How many times did I stop the vice principal and tell him somebody was picking on me? How many times did I go to my mother and have to get in line behind a Dalmatian with worms? And as far as my dad goes—forget it. All he wanted to hear was the sound of the cash register.

"Remember, Teddy. People experience grief and loss in different ways. There's no right or wrong way."

"Yes, ma'am."

She wants to hug me, but I'm out of my chair and at the screen door. "Do you want to say hi to Mrs. Rafter? I'll keep an eye on the kids."

"That's very nice of you, Ted. I will say hello."

When she's inside, I head for the van, where the two boys are playing catch.

LeBraun tosses the ball to me, and it bounces off my chest.

"You get the iron glove award, man."

It's a relief to get away from Ms. Ervin. I feel like she's been poking me with a stick. I tell LeBraun, "I guess I'm not Cool Papa Bell."

"Who's he?"

"Black baseball player when there was so much segregation that there had to be a Negro League."

"He have good hands?"

"Uh-huh. And he was so fast he could hit the light switch then jump in bed before the room got dark."

LeBraun looks suspicious. "How you know about him?"

"My father told me."

At the magic word—*father*—the other boy starts to cry. LeBraun just sneers. "Here come the fuckin' waterworks again."

"What's his story?" I ask.

"He adopted by white folks, then they up and die and the relatives are all, 'I don't even like chop suey.' So the next thing you know he in the system. Somebody take him, though. For good I mean. He all clean and exotic. They's ten thousand little knuckleheads like me. I be lucky somebody don't beat my ass to death and toss me on the side of the road."

"Let's go, boys." I watch Ms. Ervin herd them like ducks. They scramble into the van. She slides the heavy door shut. "You call me, all right, Ted? Any little thing, you call me."

"Yes, ma'am."

She walks back to me. "How's C.W. doing? We had an appointment and he didn't show up. I don't have time for that."

"He's the most popular kid at school."

She snorts, but wants to believe it.

I open the door for her, then wait until she pulls away. I'm still thinking about Cool Papa Bell. He really was an amazing athlete. Dad told me all about him while we drove to minor league ballparks. He made sure we got there after the seventh-inning stretch because then admission was free.

That late in the game, we could almost always sneak

into the boxes behind the dugout. He'd pick up a program somebody had thrown away so he could harass the players by name ("Don't just stand there, Sanchez. Get around on it!"). Then he'd rag on the umpire while I sank lower and lower in the seat we hadn't paid for.

That was his idea of a father-son night out.

CHAPTER

4

I have another bad night. I toss and turn. The lions make a circle around my bed and growl at something out there in the dark. In a dream, my parents crawl out of their graves. Finally I hear Astin get up, and then a little later the sound of his motorcycle. I guess I go back to sleep, but it's nine or so before I stagger downstairs.

Mrs. Rafter is still in the kitchen, wearing crinkly-looking gold pants and a gold zippered top. She looks like a big souvenir from Fort Knox.

There's syrup and butter on the table, a big blue bowl beside the stove.

"Where is everybody?" I ask.

"Bob's at church, Astin's riding with some friends, and C.W.'s playing basketball. So I'm making waffles. It'll be our secret."

"I'm not all that hungry."

She turns around, holding the spatula like a wand. "You've never had waffles like these, Teddy. You fold the egg whites in separately. I'll bet your mother never did that."

I pull out a chair. "My mother fed everybody out of the same box. Me, the animals, Dad, everybody."

"Probably she was busy."

"You can say that again."

"Do you want coffee, honey?"

"Sure."

"And some milk. For your bones."

I start to get up.

"No, no," she says. "I'll get it."

She gives me a heavy mug and a tall plastic glass with oranges on it. Then she pours batter and closes the lid of a very old-looking waffle iron.

"Don't let me eat any more," she says. "I'm going to Curves at eleven."

"Okay."

"Did your mom belong to a gym or anything?"

I shake my head. "She didn't go out much."

"I don't know what I'd do without Curves," Mrs. Rafter says. "There are four or five gals I see there all the time that I just really like. We don't call each other on the phone and I'm not sure I know their last names, but we've all got time on our hands and a person can only watch so much *Oprah*. . ." She lets the sentence drift away and gets busy coaxing a perfect waffle off the griddle.

And it actually is just about perfect. I tell her, "This is really good."

She comes all the way around the table and tries to play with my hair, then retreats back to the counter, where she worries little bits of dried batter off the waffle iron. "If I took you to get a haircut, would you like that? I'm thinking of a different kind," she says. "Something spunkier. Bob won't like it. Anything longer than a buzz cut is just another sign of the end times. But what does he know? He's about as sensitive as a two-by-four. If he ever had a feeling, he'd probably hit it with a hammer. Has he got my name on his big fat arm? No, he's got *Semper Fi*. And just try talking to him about anything."

Mrs. Rafter sighs and moves her coffee cup around. "Ms. Ervin says that you're starting to talk about what happened to your parents." She drips a little syrup onto a broken piece of waffle and pops it in her mouth. "It'll get easier, Teddy. It's not like you forget, but you just don't remember all the time. I don't remember all the time."

"Remember what?"

"I lost my baby. My Toby. Bob wasn't what you'd call supportive, but I wanted what I wanted. Everything seemed fine right up to the day I went in the hospital, and then it was one complication after another. Oh, Teddy, sometimes I'm so empty inside."

I push my chair back. Fast.

Mrs. Rafter asks, "Are you finished, honey?"

"Yes, ma'am. And now I've got—"

"Come with me, Teddy. There's something I want to show you."

"Mrs. Rafter—"

"Barbara."

"Barbara, breakfast was great. Really. But—"

"This will just take a minute. I wouldn't want to have to tell Ms. Ervin you were being difficult."

"Honest, I'm sorry about your baby and all, but—"

"Don't disappoint me, Teddy. Don't make me call somebody. There are foster children in this town who are sleeping in basements with rats."

I don't want to, but I follow her down the hall past all those pictures of Mr. Rafter in uniform. I stop and look at the one where he's standing by a Jeep. What if I just made a run for it?

"Teddy!"

When I get to the bedroom, she's already in a rocker. It's about ten o'clock. The shades are down, and there's a fat candle burning.

She says, "Ms. Ervin likes you, Teddy."

"Barbara..." My voice kind of breaks, and I can't finish.

Up comes the index finger. "Shh. She thinks you're unusually sensitive. I think you're sensitive, too, Teddy. I think you'd understand things other boys might not. C.W.'s not somebody to confide in, and Astin's just a big noisy boy in tight pants."

My eyes adjust to the gloom. A door leads to their bathroom, where I can see a damp towel hanging on a hook. There's a big bed that's not even made. And there's a cradle, the old-fashioned kind with the curved rockers.

Mrs. Rafter holds out her arms. "Would you bring her to me, Ted."

"Who?" I sound like Woodsy the Owl. "Bring who?"

"Little Noodle." She nods toward the cradle. "She's had her nap."

"Mrs. Rafter, I don't think—"

"Please. Don't make me get up."

So I cross the swamp-colored carpet. Finally I look down and see her. Or it.

"Isn't she beautiful, Ted?"

I think its name is Nora Newborn. I think I've seen it in a Toys Я Us ad on television. It's diapered, it's slightly wrinkled. It's supposed to be lifelike, but if you ask me it's corpselike. I pick it up by a foot.

"Careful." Mrs. Rafter frowns. "Hold her in your arms. Support her little head. Now let me have her."

I can't wait to be rid of it. The skin is cool and doughy, like zombies' feet. I hand her over and step back. As far back as I can.

She says, "Bob thinks I'm stupid and that I'm living in a dream world." She unzips her gold top and there's her bra. It's huge and all crisscrossed with straps, guy wires, and rigging.

There's even a trapdoor, and when she undoes that, a big nipple pops out like an accusing finger. Then she presses Noodle's plastic head to her chest.

"But who," she asks, "does it hurt?"

I don't know what to do. Much less what to say. The front door opens, then closes with a bang.

"It's…somebody," I hear myself say. "I should go."

She just plants a kiss on Noodle's made-in-Taiwan forehead.

I run all the way to the Gold Line station. There's only one place I want to be right now.

* * *

On the ride south, I'm kind of sick at my stomach. My mouth tastes like old pennies. My mother was odd, but she wasn't psycho. If she'd had something called Little Noodle, it would've been a dachshund.

People doze or talk on their phones. Somebody with an old school boom box gets on, turns it way down, and leans his ear against it. At the Arroyo station, a man watches the woman he's been talking to walk south carrying plastic bags in each hand; then he holds up a little portable radio and I can hear Vin Scully, the voice of the Dodgers.

I let myself think about my parents.

My dad was a baseball fanatic. He always had a game on the radio. His bedtime stories were all about mistakes: Enos Slaughter scores from first, beating Johnny Pesky's lousy relay throw (Game 7, '46). Bill Buckner lets Mookie Wilson's dribbler get by him, and the winning run scores (Game 6, '86).

My mother's stories were about animals—how giraffes in captivity lick the fence when they're upset, why hurt animals in the wild don't whine and carry on because it'd attract predators, how birds that migrate have to learn and then remember the route because it isn't hardwired into their brains.

Every now and then I'd hear about the day she was walking home from the store with some groceries and my dad pulled up on a little Yamaha. She said how long his legs were and he said how cute she was.

I have to sit back and take a couple of deep breaths.

A family of four gets on. The father stares out the window; the daughter opens a book, then fumbles with her glasses; her little brother crawls into his mother's lap. He settles in with both arms around her neck, but as he dives deeper into sleep, his arms slip loose and hang over the back of the seat, limp as vines.

That about does me in. I've got that photograph in my wallet. But I don't take it out. It'll just make things worse.

The Gold Line ends downtown. It's only a few hundred yards from that platform to the bus stop in front of Union Station. Then twenty minutes on the DASH bus.

I'm first off that, first in line to get the student discount, first to push through the turnstile. The zoo is big and green. It reminds me of Africa. At least all the bamboo does. Not the corny asphalt trails or the caterpillar-like trams with the loudspeakers.

I still feel more at home. I like the heavy air—biting and sour. Most people hold their noses, but it tells me things: *I live here. This is my territory. Don't come any closer.*

I stand outside the new enclosure for sea lions. Huge windows give everybody an underwater view, and up a dozen stairs there's plenty of room for the pups to lie in the sun.

I say hello to them, but they're too busy diving and having fun to reply. My dad didn't like the sea lions or the seals. He said they loved their jailers too much. He wouldn't watch them bark and clap their flippers and roll over for fish at the two o'clock public feeding. He told me that the reason I didn't have any brothers and sisters was that he couldn't breed in captivity.

A hundred yards away, the flamingos squawk and bend their long necks to hunt under one wing for something that's aggravating them. One of them spots me and walks toward the iron railing.

"Your pants are awful," he says.

"They're Ralph Lauren."

"They're brown. You should wear brighter colors."

"Are you guys okay?"

He shrugs. "I miss flying. How are you?"

"I'm having a little trouble. I kind of miss my folks."

"Really? My mom's in Florida, I think. Eggs are definitely the way to go."

A little girl standing just behind me says, "Daddy, why's that boy laughing?"

Her father isn't quite sure what to do. He likes having the tall colorful bird right up close, but he's not so sure about me.

So I move on. I don't go by the chimps, because they all jabber at once. My mother told me a story once about chimp wars. A couple of troops of males would meet on neutral turf and throw it down. That's how researchers finally figured out the weird female-to-male ratio they ran into every now and then; a lot of the males had been killed. Mom said Jane Goodall hated to think her beloved chimps could do something like that. But they could and did.

Giraffes don't make war. I like seeing a real giraffe instead of the one in the backyard. I stand by their big enclosure, and the dominant female strolls my way.

"Teddy. How nice of you to drop by."

Giraffes are always polite and kind of upper-class.

She leans as close as she can and bats her lashes at me. "You seem shorter. Or maybe that's because you look so awful."

"I'm just upset, I guess. You know what happened… The accident and all."

She nods as only a giraffe can nod. "That was a shame.

They were young."

"It's not like they were perfect. No way were they perfect, but. . ."

"Nobody's perfect, Teddy." She leans a little to her left. "See that big oaf over there? Nobody can go into that corner by the boulders because it's his precious corner. He has to eat first. He has to go inside first at night. But nobody wants to see him die. Wasn't it rather like that with your parents?"

"Sort of, yeah."

"Just being alive at all is pretty much a combination of good and bad, Teddy. This is a bad part. If you can be patient, it'll get better."

"Were you patient," I ask, "when you were captured and brought here?"

"It was terrible at first; then I got used to it."

"It's kind of terrible where I am."

By now there are people all around me. A dozen fathers holding up their kids while the giraffe nibbles at my hair.

I say, "Look, I'm just going to, you know, wander around a little, I guess."

"Go visit the lions. All boys like predators."

"All right. I will. Thanks."

I make my way through the little crowd. I'm sure people

are looking at me and wondering, but I don't care.

When I get to the big cat pavilion, the male lion stands up, shakes his mane, and makes one of those low, coughing roars.

"Theodore," he says, "what are you doing here?"

"I just came by to say hello."

"Oh, there's more going on than that. You can tell me. I'm king of the beasts."

"Well, okay." Finally I take the picture of my parents out of my wallet and hold it up. "Can you see this?"

"Are you kidding? There are three people—a male and a female and a cub. The male has his arm around the female, they're both smiling, and the little one's asleep."

"Well, they died. And I'm living in this foster home, and the lady there has this doll and she's pathetic, and her husband is this old military guy and he's pathetic, and sometimes I'm just so lonely."

"What you need, Theodore, is a pride. If you can get some females to hunt for you, that's all the better. Nothing beats lying around under a tree while the girls work. But a few young guys—that's okay, too. Promise me you won't spend too much time by yourself—the hyenas will get you."

"Son?"

I look up to see two park guards in their blue uniforms.

Behind them are a dozen people.

"Are you okay?" The big guard has his hand on my shoulder. "It says right there you can't feed the animals."

"I wasn't feeding the animals."

"You could have fooled me. Those lions never get that close to the moat, and if they do, they don't stay there unless somebody's throwing food."

"I was just showing them this picture."

He reaches for the photo in my hand. "Who are these people?"

"My parents."

"You're showing the lions a picture of your parents?" He starts to lead me through the crowd. "They around here somewhere?"

"No, I'm by myself."

"Did you drive?"

"I took the bus. And before that the Gold Line. I live in Pasadena now."

"It's nice up there. I've got family in Pasadena."

Down in the enclosure, the lion has his back to everything.

"You're not on anything, are you?" the guard asks.

"Like drugs? Are you kidding? I don't mind leaving. I know that's what you want me to do."

"Do we need to walk with you?"

"No. I know where the gate is."

They get on either side of me. "I think we'll just walk with you anyway."

CHAPTER 5

The next day I'm dozing when Astin comes in. He's limping, and his jeans are torn.

"Hey, man," he says. "Did you even make it to school? I didn't see you all day."

"I was late, but I made it."

"You were dead to the world this morning."

"I'm still trying to get over Little Noodle."

His grin is huge. "Is that far out or what?"

I sit up and put both feet on the floor. The clock says it's the middle of the afternoon. "Is she going to keep doing that?"

Astin opens the top drawer of his IKEA dresser and paws through it.

"If she tries, here's the drill—you see that look on her face and she starts talking about her womb, you're out the door."

"But she told me if I was difficult, she'd call Ms. Ervin."

"No way is she calling anybody, Teddy. What's she gonna say—that you wouldn't play dolls with her? Look at it this way: she hasn't got her hand in your pants, she's not drunk, and she's not stoned. But now you're an official foster kid. You get the I'VE SEEN LITTLE NOODLE T-shirt."

"I about lost it. That bra of hers looks seaworthy."

Astin cackles, then clutches at his side. "Don't make me laugh; my ribs hurt."

"What happened?"

"I was helping a buddy of mine work on his rice burner, and when I took it out for a spin, I had a little wreck. I wasn't going very fast. I'm all right." He starts tugging at his belt. "I'm going to change my pants, then get something to eat. Come with me."

"I just keep seeing those boobs of hers. I may never eat again."

"I'm buying. I hate to eat alone."

"Call Megan."

"She's making puppets for that AP English class you guys are in. C'mon, we'll take the chopper. Get you some street cred."

"Okay, I guess. I sure don't want to stay here."

Outside, Astin points to the tarp on his motorcycle. "Help me with this."

I tell him, "I feel sorry for her. Do you feel sorry for her?"

"For Barbara? Are you kidding? If I feel sorry for anybody, it's Bob."

We lift at the same time, and the tarp billows a little.

"Give it a shake and then stand still."

I watch him come toward me, one fold after another. He brushes at the tarpaulin, fusses with the corners. I go over what Astin told me: she starts in with the waffles and the womb; I'm out the door. If it works for him, it'll work for me.

I follow him into the garage, where he opens the trunk of Mrs. Rafter's Saturn and stows the folded cover. Then he wants me to look too.

"What'd your old man drive?" he asks.

"Subaru."

"What'd his trunk look like?"

"Afghanistan."

He opens a varnished box with brass hinges. There's a fire extinguisher, yellow jumper cables, red flares, one of those aluminum blankets, bottled water, a see-through sandwich bag full of folded maps, and some kind of walkie-talkie.

"She's afraid of earthquakes," he says.

So there's Barbara with her doll wondering if the overpass is going to fall on her before she gets to Curves. Oh, God.

Astin leads me back outside and pats the motorcycle like it's a big pet.

"Harley Shovelhead, S&S engine, and a Boyd front end. I drove all over hell and gone to find stuff. And what I couldn't find I made. This thing is so lean and mean I've had guys tell me it won't run 'cause it hasn't got enough parts."

There's not much room for paint, but the gas tank is the deepest blue I have ever seen. "It's nice."

"You bet your ass it's nice. This baby and I go to Daytona Speed Week next year and win some prizes." He mounts up, hands me a helmet, grabs the handlebars, and leans back. "Get on."

I step back. "No way am I putting my arms around you."

"Just grab hold of my jacket. Nobody'll see you,

anyway. We'll be going too fast."

He turns the key, and we're gone. Dry leaves fly up behind us like a wake. I don't much want to, but I have to hang on to something because we're up to at least fifty miles per hour just like that.

"You okay?" he shouts.

"Yeah." Actually I'm a little scared, but I'm not going to tell him that. And it's nothing like when those three jocks turned me upside down in a trash can. This is kind of fun.

He leans us into a turn. "Know how to drive?" he yells.

"A car, yeah."

"Not one of these?"

When I shake my head, my helmet bumps against his. The wind grabs part of our conversation.

"Get you started in a nice big parking lot where you can't run into anything."

"I'd just fall over, break something."

"So I fix it."

"I meant something of mine. Like a leg."

"Tell everybody you laid it down, lucky to get out alive. Chicks love war stories. Show 'em your scars."

He slows down and pulls up to a stoplight. We're

first when the light changes, and he keeps revving the engine.

"Hey!"

I glance to my right, where a white standard poodle, groomed like he's up for Best in Show, has his head out the window.

I reply, "Hey, yourself."

He nods toward the driver, a woman with too much Botox in her lips. He says, "All I do is cruise up and down this street with Ms. Fancy Pants, so I know what I'm talking about. Watch out for a cop parked behind that Shell station up ahead."

"Thanks. Are you all right?"

"So-so. I wasn't bred just to ride around in a Lexus, but I can't complain. How about you and your boyfriend?"

"Hey, it's not like that."

"Sorry. I got a look at myself in the mirror this morning. Do you believe this haircut?"

On the green, I lean forward and tell Astin to take it easy for a block or so.

"Why?"

"Just a hunch."

Sure enough, not thirty seconds later there's the snout

of a black-and-white cruiser peeking out, then the driver holding a radar gun.

"Too cool, Teddy!" says Astin. "You can ride with me anytime."

We pull into the parking lot of Blue's Burgers, which pretty much straddles the dividing line between San Marino and Pasadena.

I think of those chimp wars Mom told me about because guys from Alhambra and Santa Mira and Pasadena and Arcadia mill around in their school jackets. It's like a watering hole in Africa, too. There's a lot of sniffing and snorting and jostling for position.

I've heard about Blue's, but I've never been here. My parents didn't eat out, and, anyway, all I needed was to show up somewhere cool with my mommy and daddy. I guess I could have ridden down on my bicycle, but why? People who go to Blue's want to see and be seen. I wanted to be invis ible.

Astin squats down beside the motorcycle, takes a handkerchief out, and wipes the chrome. He talks without looking at me. "Pretty soon, Bob's going to take you off KP and give you the garbage detail."

"Did I do something wrong?"

"Nope. It's a promotion." He glances up at me. "You know why Bob's always out in that workshop, don't you?" Astin doesn't wait for me to answer. "She wants to adopt, but he doesn't. She gets pretend kids and he gets a check every month, but she won't let it go. So he's just like, '*Adios.*'" He wipes his hands carefully. "I'd pity any baby she ever got her hands on. She's more screwed up than my mom, and that's saying something."

I ask, "What'd your mom do?"

He doesn't look at me. "Drugs, booze, any guy in a leather jacket."

"Do you ever see her?"

"I think she's dead."

"I know mine is."

"Lucky us. Let's eat."

I follow him at top speed. He pushes past everybody. Slips in between two customers leaning on the grimy-looking counter. "Billy! Two of everything."

A man in a sport coat says, "I beg your pardon."

Astin doesn't bother with him. He's grinning at the guy on his right, who has a shaved head and one of those beard-and-mustache combinations that looks like a toilet brush.

"Do you," he asks, "beg my pardon too?"

"Get lost."

"And," says somebody from the back of the pack, "get in line like everybody else."

"Well, that's not going to happen." Astin turns, puts both elbows on the counter, and leans back. Standing like that makes his chest stick out. Male prairie chickens do this during mating season. I don't think I'll tell him that.

"And it's not going to happen," he says, "because I've been coming here forever. I look out over you guys, and I don't know any of you. So don't tell me to get in line at my own place. Okay?" He meets one set of eyes after another. Then he says, "Good." And he turns around.

In the dog world, Astin would be called a dominant biter.

Then I hear, "Somebody ought to kick your ass."

Now there's fear-based aggression in the mix.

"But nobody's going to." Astin pulls a handful of napkins out of a bent dispenser.

"We might."

There's a couple of grimy guys who look like they've been digging a grave. They wear the same kind of sunglasses and the same kind of Timberland boots with the laces undone. They're probably on the football team, and they're probably not very good.

Astin strolls toward them. Gets close. Too close. Right into their space.

"Just wait your turn," says the big one, who's wearing an Alhambra High T-shirt.

"No."

From behind the counter, a cook pleads, "Don't cause trouble, Astin."

He doesn't even turn around. "I would never do that, Billy. I would never cause trouble for you. If it comes to that, we'll take it down the street. So here's the question—is it going to come to that?"

Alhambra says, "There's two of us, and your buddy doesn't look like much."

I don't move. Astin glances at me. "Leave him out of this," he says. "It'd take more than you two to make me need backup." Then he opens his hands, shows them the palms first, then the other side so they can see he's not hiding a big ring or brass knuckles or a bomb. "Just good old-fashioned fists," he says. "We're not gang-bangers."

I know what it's like to be on the receiving end of this, and my stomach turns over a time or two.

"Astin!" The cook pounds on the counter with the palm of one hand. "Your food's ready. Come and get it."

"Fellas?" He appeals to his foes. "Last chance for glory."

They look at him, then at each other. And then away. One of them grumbles, "Next time, fucker."

Astin just laughs, slaps down a twenty, and takes the

cardboard tray. I fall in beside him, and we head for the nearest table.

I ask, "What was that about, anyway?"

"I didn't want to wait in line."

I shake my head. "You're really something."

He shrugs. "I just like to mix it up, you know? And I'm not scared of getting beat on. Most guys are. They're afraid they won't be pretty anymore."

Astin puts the food down. He settles in, sitting backward on a folding chair and putting both elbows on the scarred wood.

"What's it like to be you?" I ask.

"It's okay, I guess. Megan says I'm totally predictable."

I watch those two guys from Alhambra stop by their truck, turn around, and stare at us. Glare at us. I tell him, "I should have stepped up before. I should have said I'd fight, too. But I was scared."

"Do you know how?"

"To fight? Get serious."

"Then you'd just be in the way, wouldn't you? For the record, though, and we're just talking here—when was the last time you were heads up with somebody?"

"That I got in a fight or that I just got hassled?"

"Who hassled you?"

"Mostly this guy in my old high school. Scott McIntyre."

"Not the douche-bag quarterback who led the Titans to a memorable three-and-eleven season?"

"I didn't go to any games, but yeah. That Scott McIntyre. He and his crew never left me alone. I mean never. I mean every day."

"I hate that shit. If I'm riding and I see some like middle school kids throwing it down and it's three against one, I am off the bike and right in their faces."

"Astin, you just picked on two guys you never saw before."

"That's different. They were bigger than me. Together they were, anyway. That would've been a fair fight. You against McIntyre, there's no way. He was a jock and you're... what were you, anyway?"

"I sold kitty litter."

"There you go." He waves at somebody he knows who's sitting a dozen yards away. Then he asks, "Were you just smarter than him or what?"

"Than Scott? Anybody's smarter than Scott. No, I was just one of those guys who gets picked on. Even in first grade I always took a lot of heat about my parents' smelly old store."

"First grade's a bitch."

"And there were a couple of things that sort of followed me around."

"Yeah, like what?"

"Just stupid things."

"Like hitting gunpowder with a hammer?"

"You did that?"

"Or setting your teacher's briefcase on fire?"

There's nobody around and they probably wouldn't care, anyway, but I still lean in. "Like in grade school I was at this party and nobody wanted to, you know, be my partner for Seven Minutes of Heaven, so I kind of trashed this desk, and then a couple of years ago I got caught sitting in some girl's car."

"Trying to hot-wire it? It's not like in those old movies. You have to know what you're doing."

"No, I was hoping she'd come out to get the mail or walk her dog or something, and I'd say, 'Why don't you like me? I never did anything to you.' I guess I wanted to start over or something.

"But time goes by and nothing happens, so I get in their car instead, in the passenger side, and...I don't know. Her dad comes out, and there I am, and he starts yelling. Then she comes out and says, 'He's this creep from my school,' and the next thing I know the cops are on their way."

"Did they take you in?"

I shake my head.

"They took me in."

"For sitting in somebody's car?"

He stabs a French fry into a pool of ketchup as he talks. "Nah. I was about eleven. You know how weird the Rafters are sometimes, so I'd go out and look in normal people's windows. Not at girls or anything. I just wanted to watch normal people eat dinner or play Monopoly. It just killed me when they played Monopoly. And the stupid cop called me a perv and gave me the Peeping Tom lecture and said if I wasn't careful, I'd be on this list for the rest of my life and nobody would want me in their neighborhood, blah blah blah. I think that's when I started hating cops."

"I guess I was lucky. Mine was one of those K-9 cops and his dog loved me. So while this German shepherd is licking me all over, he said if I'd promise to behave myself, he wouldn't call my dad."

"Lucky you. Bob had to come and get me, and I caught hell on the way home. I was grounded for like two months."

I make a little ketchup pool of my own. "I was always kind of grounded, but I pretty much did it to myself. I mean as far as friends and stuff went, after a while I just kind of gave up."

"They come and they go, man."

That makes me look up. "Who does?"

"Friends. I'm riding with guys now I didn't even know six months ago. Another six months and most of them will have turned over."

"What about kids at school? You know everybody."

"To say hi to. Big deal. Let's see how tight we are once I age out and they go to college and stuff."

He takes a big bite of cheeseburger and chews like he's mad. Then he glances over my shoulder. "Wow."

"What?"

"This babe behind you. Check it out."

"My mother told me not to stare."

"Teddy, she wore those pants so guys would look at her. Wait, don't move. She's coming this way."

I take a sip of Coke, I watch Astin light up like a neon sign, then the girl is past us.

I tell him, "She's not as cute as Megan."

He stops with a fistful of fries halfway to his mouth then shoves the little greasy bag my way. "Did she ever show you her hunting knife?"

"Megan? No way."

"She says the next time some English teacher asks about those two roads that diverged in a yellow wood, she's going to open a vein."

"I really like Megan."

"I like her, too. That's why it's gonna be hard to graduate. Then I'm just a guy who works in a garage, and she's still the little rich girl living large with her single mom." He takes the plastic lid off his Coke, drinks straight from the cup, then chews the ice.

"Where's her dad, anyway?" I ask.

Astin makes a big, plane-taking-off gesture with his hand. "Gone. Ran off with his secretary. Not very original, huh? But left them with *beaucoup* dollars. So Melanie turns into a spa junkie.

"Who's Melanie?"

"Megan's mom. She's gone right now, up to her ass somewhere in Magic Mud."

Astin takes off his watch cap, sniffs it, puts it back on again, and blurts, "Is everybody a freaking orphan? Megan's almost always by herself; about every twenty minutes Belle's folks fly off somewhere with a bunch of Doctors Without Borders; and Wanda's folks won a chunk of money playing the lottery, bought a big-assed motor home, and they haven't been seen since. What were your parents like? Did they at least stay home?"

"Are you kidding? All they did was stay home. They made me work really hard, and what I was supposed to do with my life was graduate high school, then take over the business. So I kind of hated them, or I thought I did. Now I'm not so sure."

Astin shakes his head. "I always thought it'd be great if I had folks and they had a plan for me."

"Oh, yeah. I can just see you behind the counter explaining the merits of the Super Pooper Scooper."

As he watches me eat the last of my hamburger, a big dog comes bounding our way. His owner, a short blonde wearing a T-shirt covered with what look like meteors, is already on her feet.

The dog sticks his long nose into my palm and says, "I'm supposed to be licking the cute guy."

"Thanks a lot."

"You know what I am?" asks the dog.

"Sure, a border collie."

"I'm a pimp. Cindy only got me to meet guys. She points to one, I run over, she's all, 'Oh, I'm so sorry,' they get to talking, and pretty soon they exchange phone numbers. I might as well have a fur hat and a few gold teeth." He looks behind him. "Here she comes, so pet me fast."

I lean down and put my face against his.

"Now you're breaking my heart," he says. "You don't have sheep, do you?"

"No."

"I'd herd anything. I'd herd cats if you wanted me to."

I shake my head.

"Ducks? Anything. Please. We'll go into business. I can find lost children. I live in Arcadia. Eleven seventeen Rosewood. I'll leave the back door open."

Just then, Cindy arrives.

"Oh," she says. "I'm so sorry. He gets away from me sometimes."

Astin stands up so she can get a look at all of him. "Not a problem." He holds out a hand. "I'm Astin. This is Ted."

She doesn't even bother to look at me. She's seen enough from a distance. I play with the dog while Astin writes down a phone number. I try to remember what he talks to her about in case I ever have a conversation with a girl. But it's nothing special: where she goes to school, her part-time job at the mall, his motorcycle. Like my English teacher would say, I guess—it's not content, it's style.

I point toward the parking lot. "I'll meet you."

"Be right there, Teddy."

The dog is mad at me and looks the other way, so I go and lean on the Harley. I think, *So this is Blue's.* People talked about it like it was the Parthenon.

Now I've got a Blue's story of my own—I almost got in a fight there once. Yeah. These two jerks from Alhambra. But this buddy of mine kind of stepped up, and I didn't have to get a bloody nose over nothing.

This buddy of mine.

Astin comes jogging up. "Cindy works out."

"I'll bet."

"Did you see those abs?"

"Everybody saw those abs, Astin."

"Yeah, but I'm the one with her phone number."

"That you know of."

He swings one leg over and starts the Harley. "So you're saying..."

"You probably aren't her first boyfriend."

"Yeah, you're right. You got condoms at home?"

"God, no."

He eases us onto Huntington. "I'll pick some up. Good call, Teddy." He reaches over and around and knocks on my helmet.

I like riding toward home behind Astin. There's a bar to lean back on, and since we're not going very fast, I put my hands in my pockets. When we come to a stoplight, I put my feet down, too.

Astin's all in leather, and I've got on a windbreaker and khakis that never need ironing. Scott McIntyre called me a retard, and I probably look like one.

But I like it, anyway. The ride, I mean. People look at us—guys, espe cially. It's Astin they admire, not me. Or maybe not. Maybe they'd just like to park their big dumb cars and tag along like I'm doing.

I lean with him as we make the turn at Wayne Street. He knows how to use the clutch and make the pipes rumble even when we're not going very fast.

"Hey! Isn't that C.W.?"

Sure enough. He's sitting on the retaining wall at the corner. Every now and then he dribbles his basketball.

Astin glides right up in front of him. "What's happening."

C.W. slides off the wall, glances around, and comes right up to us.

"Guess who just gave his statement to the police?"

"What statement?"

"I'm playin' ball with the brothers down at Marengo when four hairy guys in an Acura pull up. The next thing I hear is *pop, pop, pop,* and everybody but me is facedown on the asphalt."

Astin turns off the engine. "They shot at you?"

"They shot at somebody. Scared the crap out of me. I'm telling you, man. If I could stay as pale as I was an hour ago, I'd get a scholarship to the University of

Alabama." He tugs at his baggy shirt. "I'm through with this ghetto shit."

I dismount and point to the motorcycle. "Get on. Ride home with Astin."

He shakes his head. "They not lookin' for me in particular. Probably one of them's sister said a brother made fun of her mustache, so they all get their pieces and start drivin' around."

I tell him, "So go home and lay low."

"All right. Maybe you're right. You gonna be okay?"

"What are they going to do, shoot me for being drab?"

He holds out his fist, and I tap it with mine. He says, "Thanks, man."

"I'll come back for you," Astin says.

"Get serious. It's like four blocks."

"No, Teddy," he says. "I'll be back."

CHAPTER 6

I'm on my way to school when I see Gus and his dog, Paperboy. They're on the corner with the stoplight. Gus has a cup in one hand and a sign around his neck: HELP ME FEED MY DOG. Girls stop to pet Paperboy and usually drop a quarter or two into the soggy Starbucks cup.

I haven't seen them for a couple of months. They used to camp up by the trailhead that leads to Mount Lowe, then pan handle Santa Mira for a while.

When I give Gus a dollar, he stares at me. He's dirty, and with that beard he could be the ninth-place finisher in the Walt Whitman look-alike contest.

"Hey," he says, "I know you."

"Ted. From the pet shop."

He points a grimy finger at me. "Dog Eat Dog World, right?"

"Close enough."

"What're you doing down here?"

"My folks are on vacation, so I'm staying with a friend."

Gus holds out his cup as the students pile up waiting for the light.

"What really happened?" asks Paperboy.

"Car accident."

"I remember your parents," he says. "They treated you like a... well, you know."

"I guess."

"Did they leave you anything?"

"Not much."

"That's tough. What's next for you now—Africa?"

I shake my head. "I have to finish school first."

"So where are you staying?" the dog asks.

"With some people who take care of strays."

"Like the pound?"

"Kind of."

"Can you get adopted?"

"Probably not. I'm pretty old."

"So then they put you to sleep."

"I just age out. Then I'm on my own."

He nods. "That's cool. Excuse me." Paperboy lays his ears back and growls as two or three boys in school jackets lunge at Gus and pretend to grab at his cup of small change.

Paperboy says, "I'd like to tear their throats out."

"I know what you mean."

"You could come with us, Teddy. We're down by the L.A. River. It's not bad. Ducks to chase. Place to sleep. Something new every day. Even the voices in Gus's head are different."

"I'm okay where I am for now." I watch Gus rattle his cup. Two ninth-grade girls stop and pet Paperboy, who lets his big red tongue hang out. "Gus shares the money with you, doesn't he?"

"Most of the time. We do okay. People think he ought to get a job, but with me along, they cut him some slack. He feeds me because I'm his meal ticket."

Before I can say good-bye and head for school, Paperboy jumps up and puts his paws on my chest. I'm five four and a half and he's a big dog—wiry-haired and barrel-chested. His muzzle is partly gray, his coat heavy and a little matted.

"Be careful," he says.

"Well, sure. I'm just going to biology and English."

"Don't 'Well, sure' me, Teddy. There are lots of crows around. That's never good."

I put my nose to his. "I didn't know you were superstitious."

"Who's superstitious? I know what I know."

On my way to Mr. Fowler's class, I pass Valerie Wynne, Pamela Choi, and Robin Hollander, the power brokers of tenth grade. (Megan is in eleventh. Astin's going to graduate.) Valerie, Pamela, and Robin are, as my art teacher used to say, at the center of the painting. The rest of us—the stoner with the ring in her nose, the boy with the droopy Mohawk, the girl in the wheelchair—are just background. We might as well be trees and clouds.

If Valerie decides that a new teacher is okay, then everybody can like him and answer questions in class. If Pamela hates him, though, everybody has to hate him or be uncool to the ninth power. Like I care. I enrolled here already uncool to the ninth power.

I watch them stand there, preen, and rant. They are the kind of girls Megan was talking about that first day I met her and Astin outside the cafeteria: too cool to phone. I wonder if they've got a whole different set of sense organs or just a different way of processing sensory data, like elephants and their infrasonic sound waves or dolphins and their sonar.

I'll probably never know. They are like a whole other species.

Mr. Fowler is my biology teacher. He's big and bald and can't shut up about himself. He worked for the Centers for Disease Control and Prevention in Atlanta. And then guess what? He got real sick and had to be flown to the City of Hope, just outside Los Angeles.

When he got well, he stayed in L.A. and presto, changed someone into Mrs. Fowler. Then had some little Fowlers. On his desk is a picture of his wife and two kids and a cat in sunglasses. My mother hated stuff like that. She thought it was disrespectful, and I actually kind of agree. Animals don't like it; they just put up with it.

The other day Mr. Fowler whirled around, raised both arms, and hissed, "Creatures with wings." Today he turns the lights off, punches a button, and up there on the screen is a bacterium as big as a Volkswagen.

E. coli stares like it's daring everybody to eat the mayonnaise. Mr. Fowler lectures. I watch the motes of light in a shaft of sun. "And in order to survive," he says, "it's completely adaptable."

Well, I'm at least as smart as Mr. Coli. I mean, I thought

I'd never get used to that attic and I kind of have, and I wondered if I'd ever get along with C.W. or Astin and I kind of do.

When I get to my English class, there's chaos. Somehow a bird flew in from the Pit, across the cafeteria, down a long hall, and finally in here. Girls are screaming, and boys swat at it with their books. It throws itself against the window until I get close. Then it sinks to the sill and waits for me to walk over and pick it up.

I tell Mr. Sterling, "I'll just take it outside."

"Thank you, Teddy. I'll try and restore some order in here."

A sparrow is the best hall pass ever. I just say that Mr. Sterling told me to set it free.

When I get back, it's business as usual. My English teacher is also the yearbook adviser. And because it's spring, someone from his staff is always popping in between classes with a question that just can't wait or a sample from the layout table.

Right on the floor beside my desk is a page with captions but no photographs: Cutest Couple, Pest, Drama Queen, Work in Progress. That kind of thing.

Somebody took a digital picture of me for the yearbook, but what are they going to say underneath— Unknown White Male? I wouldn't mind coming back here for a tenth reunion, though, lean and tanned, full of stories about bringing back another endangered species from the brink of extinction. Or maybe just with a job that isn't in a pet store.

Today is Presentation Day for term projects. I don't have to do that, thank God. I started so late that all I need is an extra essay.

First, Shimon Calabrese unveils his model of the Globe Theatre, which is mostly made from dry spaghetti.

"Shimon, why pasta?" asks Mr. Sterling.

"My mom's on a diet."

But he's got a laptop, too, so we get a virtual tour of the Globe and some portraits of Shakespeare, Edward de Vere, Francis Bacon, and Christopher Marlowe—the four contenders for the title of True Bard.

Marlowe is the long shot since he was stabbed to death in a brawl before some of the plays were even written. But one theory is that his death might have been faked so he could go on writing.

I was so miserable in my other school that I fantasized about faking my death, then finding a veterinarian who takes care of exotic animals and offering to work for nothing. I'd put in twelve-hour days. I'd sleep on the floor.

I even thought of going to my own funeral, standing

on a hill and looking down at the four or five people—or maybe just my parents and about eleven dogs—gathered around the grave with its empty casket.

Muriel Wegman is next. When she stands up, everyone stares at the diamond stud in her belly button. All the guys do, anyway.

She draws the blinds, turns off the fluorescent overheads, and lights a candle. Then she dons a black papier-mâché mask complete with beak and proceeds to recite "The Raven."

The mask is pretty good except for the acoustics: "Ones a pond uh midnigh dearie, wile ah bondered, weeg un wery..." Poe with a cold.

I know some real ravens who live up by Santa Mira. They liked to fly along beside me when I went on hikes by myself. They liked to hear stories about themselves: the Norse god Odin had two ravens who helped him keep an eye on the world, and grouchy old Apollo turned ravens from white to black because one told him something he didn't want to hear.

My superstitious mother believed that a raven with a red thread in its mouth meant there was going to be a fire, but more than once while I was microwaving a pizza for my dinner, I saw her spend an hour feeding baby ravens beef heart, oatmeal, and egg yolk.

When Muriel is finished ("Shelby livdud—devor-boor!"), we all applaud politely.

Mr. Sterling calls her name and Megan, who's been sitting by the window wearing some kind of long dress, stands up, pads to the candle, and blows it out. Then she unbuttons the dress and takes it off.

That makes the athletes sit up. It's not totally dark. Light seeps in around the blinds and from under the door.

I watch her drag a desk-size theater (proscenium, wings, apron, curtain) and set it up where Mr. Sterling usually sits.

Once, in my other school, an English teacher took us to a matinee at the Mark Taper Forum in downtown Los Angeles. There wasn't a curtain, so between scenes people in black glided out from the wings to carry off the flowers, push the couch back and turn it into a bed, and generally get things ready for Act Two.

The next day in class we discussed the play, pondered its meaning, and talked about our favorite parts of the performance. Well, the play was long, the actors were loud, and my favorite part was riding home on the train. But I kept those opinions to myself. When I had to say something, I claimed to like those people who came out in the dark between scenes.

The teacher, Mrs. Columbus, gushed, "Behind the scenes would be a wonderful place for someone like you to start, Ted."

"Yeah," muttered somebody from the back row, "way behind the scenes. Like out in the street."

Everybody laughed, and Mrs. Columbus tried not to.

Nobody's laughing at Megan. Her black bodysuit is skintight. There's even a snug cap to cover her hair.

Miniature footlights come on, then something from an opera. Something sad in Italian. She lets us listen to that for a little while before she disappears behind the tiny stage and says, "Today I'm presenting 'The Body as Prom King.' This is theater, okay? Just much, much smaller. And before you roll your eyes and remember those little fuzzy hand puppets you got for Christmas that ended up under the bed, I'd like to remind everyone that puppetry is an art. There's the Teatrong Mulat of the Philippines, the Bunraku puppets from Japan, Balinese and Chinese shadow puppets, just to name a few. Now—curtain up, house lights down. Here is Act One."

A pair of tiny somethings carved from Styrofoam rise center stage. One on each index finger. "Think of these organs as twins," she croons. "Lost children. *Kid*-neys." She breaks the word in half. "The legs know each other intimately; they twine and flex. The arms and hands are perfect allies. If the eyes are lonely for each other, they look in the mirror. But the kidneys are always apart."

All of a sudden I get a sharp pain in my back, right where my kidneys are. For the first time I wonder what it was like for my parents.

What was jarred loose during the accident? Did the spleen carom off the ribs? Did the stomach open like a wet sack? Did the punctured lungs collapse? Was everything flooded with blood?

As Megan makes her way through the body, I have to hold on to the desk with both hands. My liver throbs, then my trachea spasms, my heart speeds up, and when she comes to the brain, mine aches thinking of theirs shaking in their skulls as the car turns over and over and then bursts into flame.

Just before I almost pass out, Megan finishes. The lights go on, she takes a bow, and class is dismissed.

I almost can't get up. Somebody slaps me on the back of the head on his way out. "What are you, O'Connor? The freakin' Bird Whisperer?"

In the hall, it's like Megan has been waiting for me. She hugs all her girlfriends good-bye and hustles over.

"How did you do that thing with the bird?" she asks.

"He was already scared to death. I stayed calm."

"He just sat there until you picked him up. Did you learn how to do that at your parents' store?"

"At my parents' store I learned how to wash dogs." I point to the door of our English class. "I like that thing you just did. It really got to me. My parents' car rolled over. Did you know that?"

She shakes her head. "Just that they died."

I shift my books from one hand to the other. "So when you were talking about lungs and hearts and all that... well, it all just made me think about my folks and their lungs and hearts and stuff."

She puts her hand on my chest. The flat of her hand right on my sternum. Usually I'd flinch. Usually it's what somebody would do to push another person away, but not this time. This time it connects me to her.

"Oh, Teddy," she says. "You can't just sit up in that attic and think things like that."

"I don't. Really. I go out; I've got friends."

"Where do you go?"

"Well..." All I can think of is the backyard and the garbage cans. And school. And that one time with Astin.

"Exactly. And name three friends."

I'm all over that one. "You, Astin, and C.W."

"I don't count, Teddy. I'm un stable. You need a girlfriend. If you're alone too much, the hyenas will get you."

I honest to God take a step back. "What! What'd you just say?"

"I said if you're alone too much, the hyenas will get you. Don't you watch the Animal Channel?"

Her hand is still on my chest, and it's warm. Maybe even warmer.

"Hang around with boys," she says, "and all you do is brag and eat trans fats. And if you want to have a little cry, you're gay. Girls love it when boys cry, and I know just the girl."

"Megan, I don't think so."

"How can you not think so? You don't even know who she is."

"I mean I'm, uh, kind of busy."

"Doing what? Being an orphan? How much time does that take?"

"I just…I want to keep my grades up, and basically I don't date, okay?"

"It's not a date. It's having a friend who's a girl. Wanda's like two years older than you. She graduates with Astin in six weeks, and then she's leaving for New York, so it can't be a date. You're a way more interesting guy than you give yourself credit for, and she's totally fabulous. I'll set it up. You and Astin come over. Wanda and I will be there. We'll swim; I'll have stuff to eat. Don't say no or I'll cry."

CHAPTER 7

A week or so later, I'm walking down the stairs at the Rafters' when C.W. comes out of his room. "What's the big deal with Little Noodle?" he says. "Astin made it sound like somebody with an ax. It's a doll."

"Yeah, but didn't that whole scene freak you out?"

"Compared to havin' to shoplift for some foster mom who needs a hundred dollars for a new tattoo? Get serious. A few choruses of 'Rock-a-Bye-Baby' to the Noodle and I get this." He points to his polo shirt.

I'm still not used to him in his new clothes.

He grins at me. "What'd you pay for those chinos?"

"They were on sale at the Gap."

"Hey, just sing to the Noodle and you get an upgrade to Banana Republic."

"Astin and I do just fine at the Gap."

"Does he go in the dressing room with you and make sure everything's just fabulous?"

"No."

He puts his hand on my shoulder. "Teddy, man. I'm pullin' your chain here, okay? Just doin' the dozens at the undergraduate level, if you get my drift. So let's try it again. I say, 'Did he go in the dressing room with you?' and you say, 'Fuck you.'"

"I don't use the f-word."

"Okay, okay. How about I say, 'So you two go in the dressing room and he keeps dropping his keys. I sure hope you didn't pick 'em up.'"

"But that didn't happen."

C.W. laughs out loud. "You're one of a kind, Teddy. Where'd you grow up, Mars?"

"Kind of."

"Let's try this one more time. Forget Astin, okay? I know he's not gay. Let's say you get on my nerves, so I tell you, 'Iron is iron and steel don't rust; yo mama got an ass like a Greyhound bus.' What do you say?"

"Does it have to rhyme?"

"No. But if you gonna cap my rap, it has to put me in

my place, man. I just disrespected your mama."

"I'm not very good at this."

"Try, 'Yeah, well, yo mama raised you on ugly milk.'"

"I say that to you?"

"Uh-huh."

I stand up a little straighter. "Okay, but is Ugly Milk a brand, or is the milk itself just unattractive?"

C.W. laughs and drapes his arm around my shoulders as we walk toward the living room. "You're either the hippest son of a bitch I've seen in a long time or the dumbest cracker in the world."

Astin's watching TV, but he still wants to know who's the dumbest cracker in the world.

"Teddy here," says C.W.

"Leave Teddy alone, homie. Teddy's my right-hand man."

"Why don't you use your own hand, you lazy puke?"

They're both laughing when I give Astin the grammar exercise he left on my bed this morning. I tell him, "I changed a few things. You still don't know what a prepositional phrase is."

He barely glances at it. "Thanks, Teddy."

"So are you ready to go?"

"In a minute." He doesn't take his eyes off the screen, where a science-fiction movie is playing. "I want to see the thing with all the arms again." He motions to C.W. "There was a black guy, but the monster ate him first."

"Now, ain't that the way it goes, though." He saunters over to Astin. "Word on the street is you and Ted were makin' out in the Gap."

"Fuck you." He waves me toward him. "You're in this movie, too, Teddy."

"Yeah? Which one am I?"

He points. "Mr. Thoughtful there in the glasses. He's next on the menu."

"Where you guys goin'?" C.W. asks. "When you go?"

I answer for both of us. "Megan's."

"She's Belle's friend, right?"

"One of 'em," says Astin.

"Belle's cute. She was watchin' us play ball the other day."

"Teddy here's fixed up with Wanda today."

"Which one is she now?" asks C.W.

Astin cups both hands and holds them in front of his chest. "Curly hair, real white skin, big rack."

C.W. leans into me. "There you go, Slick. Live off the fat of the land. We make a player out of you yet."

"Ted! Can I see you a minute."

We all look at Mr. Rafter, who came out of nowhere.

I tell him, "Sure."

"I'm not waitin' till your movie's over. Meet me out back."

"Oh, man," says C.W. "He chewed me out yesterday for leavin' the hall light on. Now it's your turn."

Astin shakes his finger at me. "Just don't drag those garbage cans. Lift 'em. That way they last longer."

C.W. points to the screen. "Here comes the monster."

Outside, Bob is turning the trash cans so the labels face the same way. "Want to give me a hand here, Ted?"

We carry the first one out of the little corral he made for them, up the driveway, and almost to the street. Then on our way back, he says, "Let me show you something."

We skip the rest of the trash cans and go right into his workshop, which is spotless. The saw blades gleam, the drill press is immaculate, all the tools hanging on the wall have white outlines like bodies at a crime scene.

"I spend a lot of time in here," he says, "because everything is where it's supposed to be when it's supposed to be there. Are you following me here?"

"I think so."

"Sir."

"I think so, sir."

"So when you're supposed to be down for breakfast at seven thirty, that's what I mean."

"But I do come down at seven thirty."

"Five."

I look up at him. "Pardon me?"

"Seven thirty-five. That's when you came down yesterday."

"Oh."

"Measure twice; cut once. Screw up twice and you're history."

"I'll get up earlier."

"Good for you. You're not much trouble, Ted. I'll give you that. You don't whine to your social worker or give me any lip. But you can always do better."

He leads me outside again. I know what I'm supposed to say. "I can take care of the rest of these trash cans. They're not heavy."

"That's the ticket," he says. "Now, listen up—when Astin leaves in June, we're not taking another boy. That room is yours. The same goes for C.W. if he lasts that long. You two are it. Don't upset the applecart and you can age out here. Then I'm going on a cruise to Alaska: all you can eat and bears to look at through the binoculars. Barbara can come if she wants to or she can sit in her rocker with that doll. It's all the same to me."

"I understand." I pick up one of the green cans.

"Don't drag it, and it'll last longer."

"Yes, sir."

"Make sure you finish up out here before you do anything else."

"Astin and I are just going over to Megan's."

"Well, police this area first, and when you rake that little patch of dirt over there, I want to see all the lines in one direction."

Astin starts the Harley, and I climb on behind him. I used to think I was like the feral cats my mother fed behind the shop. They lived by the underpass, the parking structure, the clump of trees behind the cul-de-sac.

But I'm not a feral cat, and I wonder if I ever was. Maybe I was just a kid who was hard to like. Every now and then somebody would try, and I'd hiss and run away. But now Astin likes me a little and I can make C.W. laugh.

Astin half turns around. "How'd it go with Bob?"

"I got the workshop tour. 'Everything in its place.'"

"The poor bastard. He practically lives out there." Astin pats his pockets. "You got any money, Ted?"

"Some."

"Loan me sixty, will you? I don't want to stop by the ATM. We're late now."

"I have to go upstairs."

"So? What are you waiting for?"

I'm up and down inside of a minute. Astin stashes the three twenty-dollar bills and pops the clutch.

At the stoplight just before we turn onto Huntington, he says, "Wanda goes for younger guys, always has. When we were fourteen, she was making out with twelve-year-olds. When we were sixteen, she was driving fourteen-year-olds around."

"What do I talk to her about?"

"Whatever."

"I'm serious, Astin."

"Tell her about your folks."

"Oh, that's a good idea. 'My parents died in a fiery crash. Can I get you some barbecue?' "

"She's going to go on about how fat she is, okay? So let her and then say, 'Stop being hard on yourself.' "

"I can't tell her what to do. I just met her."

"She's fishing for a compliment. I'm telling you, man, she's yours if you want her."

I want to tell Astin I wouldn't know where to start. Instead I say, "My father made me promise I wouldn't get married, and my devoted mother told me once the only thing any woman would ever want me for is to get a piece of the business."

He twists the throttle and we spurt ahead. "You know," he shouts, "if those fuckers were alive, I'd go over there and set their house on fire."

"Too late for that. Anyway, thanks for telling me what to say to Wanda."

"Teddy, man. Relax. It's just a day at the pool with a couple of girls."

I'm not going to tell him I've never been anywhere with even one girl.

Megan and Wanda are waiting for us. Wanda's not more than an inch taller than I am; she's solid and strong when we shake hands. She's barefoot in loose pants and a V-neck top. Megan's wearing some kind of pool cover-up; she looks like a statue about to be unveiled to thunderous applause.

She kisses Astin like we're not there, so Wanda leads me toward the kitchen. "I'd tell them to get a room," she says, "but they would, and where would that leave us?"

I can hardly see the counter for all the stuff from Bristol Farms, a market so upscale that my parents went there to point at things, like they were on a field trip.

I say, "That would leave us alone with enough food for six people."

Wanda pretends to think that over. "You know, that doesn't sound all that bad."

She gets a lot of potato salad on a big spoon. "C'mon. Friends don't let friends eat alone." She hands me a napkin as she says, "My goal today is to gain five pounds and fall asleep in the sun. What's yours?"

Just to not do or say the wrong thing. But I tell her, "I don't know. Maybe I'll gain five pounds too."

"There you go. I like you already."

You wouldn't say that if you'd gone to my other school.

I take a couple of spareribs and some slaw and follow her out toward the pool with its tables and chairs and umbrellas.

Wanda balances her plate of food and her Coke, then falls onto a red chaise. Its cushions match the bougainvillea that tumbles down the nearest wall.

"What's it like at the Rafters'?" she asks.

I have to remind myself that she's just making conversation.

"It's okay, I guess."

"That thing with your parents. That had to be hard. Did a cop come to the door and everything?"

"Uh-huh."

"Wow, Teddy. Just like in the movies." She shakes her head. "Man, the things that happen to people. Astin's hair caught on fire once."

"On the way over here, he was talking about arson. What's going on with him and matches?"

She checks to see that we're out of earshot. "His parents used, and they'd get high and leave him alone or leave him alone so they could score. So he'd get out the old Biro. My dad was just waiting for him to torch the Rafters'."

"How did your dad know Astin?"

"He knew Bob from church."

"I heard your folks are seeing the sights."

"You can say that again." She chews as she shrugs. "Every week another postcard: the Grand Canyon, Pikes Peak, Mount Rushmore. Every week the same message: 'Glad you're not here!'" She leans over her plate of food. "I saw this thing on TV where they said about ninety percent of lottery winners are miserable."

"You don't look miserable."

"I'm not the lottery winner unless their motor home goes off a cliff. All they do is make the house payments; the rest is up to me. Nice, huh? You'd think I'd been some drug-addicted shoplifting nympho. Instead I got a job when I was sixteen and came home by midnight on weekends." She takes a serious bite of eggplant. "Who cares? I'm out of here the day after graduation, which of course they won't be in town for because there's a saguaro in Arizona they haven't taken a picture of." She holds out her plate. "Now, will you get me some more of everything or at least turn your back while I waddle into the kitchen?"

"Stop being hard on yourself, okay?" I rehearsed it so many times in my head that it comes out pretty smooth.

Wanda blushes just a little. "Sorry. You're right."

Just then Megan steps out onto the patio, points with a celery stick, and says, "I wish somebody would shut that dog up."

I tell her, "Give me a minute and I will."

In the kitchen Astin is busy loading up his plate. I step through the big sliding door that leads from the patio.

"How's it going with Wanda?" he asks.

"Fine."

"Do you believe the tits on her?"

"Shut up. She seems nice. She's easy to talk to."

"Teddy!"

We both glance toward the pool.

"Teddy!" says Megan. "When you come back, bring me a Perrier."

Astin says, "Tell her to get it herself, you don't work here."

"I'm going that way. It's fine."

I deliver Megan's French mountain spring water and Wanda's second helping, then head for the deep part of the yard. I pass a gardener's shack with its mower, gas cans, and clippers and find a big Irish setter, who is glad to stop barking and chat.

When I get back to the others a few minutes later, Megan asks, "How did you do that? My mom is always calling the cops."

"He's just bored. The kid got tired of him, so now if he gets to go out, it's with the mom, and all she does is go to her boyfriend's house, leave him locked in the car, and then cry. He's a bird dog. He wants to fetch. If I were him, I'd bark too."

"How do you know all that?" Megan asks.

"My mom, I guess. Stuff I read. Like...did you know dogs and wolves are the same for thirty days? Then the wolves start turning into real wolves and the dogs just stop there so they can be dogs. Otherwise they can't be around humans."

Megan sits up. "So a dog who keeps maturing turns into a wolf?"

"No way," says Astin, "does a Chihuahua turn into a wolf on day thirty-one."

"I just know what my mom said, and we can't ask her."

"Well," Megan says, "I'm going to swim before I eat."

She unzips her silver cover-up and steps out of it. Astin

puts down his plate and takes off his jeans. Underneath is a turquoise Speedo. The polo shirt goes, he shoves Megan, and they dive into the pool together.

"You know just a second ago when she dropped her robe?" asks Wanda. "She practiced it."

"Are you kidding?"

"I was there. She's got this like wall of mirrors in her bedroom, and she stood in front of it and got the move down just the way she wanted it. She is really enter taining."

"You guys have been friends a long time?"

She nods. "Since grade school."

"I've only known Astin since the Rafters. But he's a good guy. He's been really... Well, he's just a good guy."

"He cheats on Megan and steals from that garage he works for."

"Seriously?"

She nods. "Just chump change mostly. Quarts of oil, filters, crap like that."

I can feel my stomach tighten up like it used to. "Well, he doesn't steal from me."

"I'm just saying."

We eat and don't talk for a while. I make myself chew really slowly. In Santa Mira my stomach was always upset.

"You can swim, Teddy," Wanda tells me. "I'm fine here on the beach with the Greenpeace people pouring water on me."

Astin said she's just fishing for compliments, but I think she sounds really down on herself. "I thought you weren't going to do that anymore."

"Sorry."

"Anyway, I don't know how to swim."

That makes her look up. "Really?"

"My parents didn't see the point."

"Well, I know how, but whenever I get in the water, there are always unkind references to a certain Melville novel."

"Wanda!"

"That's the last time. I promise."

We watch Megan and Astin play in the pool. They dunk each other and laugh.

Wanda says, "I wouldn't be surprised if a celebrity spokesperson stepped out of the bushes and tried to sell us something."

"Run that by me again?"

"They're just so perfect, it seems like they ought to be selling something." Then she waves that sentence away. "Don't pay any attention to me. I watch too much television."

Astin hammers a beach ball out of the pool, so I go and get it for him. When I come back and sit down, Wanda says, "Megan can be vain and a pain in the ass sometimes. But she's a good friend, too. I hate being by myself, and I'm afraid of the dark. If I get freaked out, I call her and she comes over. If I need a couple hundred dollars for a few days, she goes right to the bank."

"I just loaned Astin some money."

Wanda puts down the sparerib she's been working on. "Well, kiss that good-bye. He's into Megan for eight or nine hundred. She can afford it, but it's still crummy."

She whispers the last part because the two of them are at this end of the pool. Then she says real loud, "Did Astin tell you I was going to New York in June?"

"Uh-huh. I have to go somewhere when I graduate. At eighteen, foster care is over."

She takes a big gulp of Coke. "Well, I want to go, but the whole thing scares the crap out of me. It's all the way across the country, I don't know anybody, and an apartment about the size of my butt costs two thousand a month."

"But you've got a job."

"Yeah. A guy I work for at the playhouse hooked me up. But I'm already lonely." She shifts a little and fans herself with one hand. "I started as an usher two years ago and worked my way backstage. I love set design. It's just playing house on a grand scale. I like figuring out how the sofa in act one can be the canoe in act two. And then I get to build it! What about you?"

"Well, I thought I'd just be stacking fifty-pound bags of Alpo and ringing up goldfish for the rest of my life. Now I don't know."

Just then, Megan and Astin start kissing like there's no tomorrow.

Wanda sits up. "That's my cue to show you around. This house is really something. "

I follow Wanda into the kitchen, where she points. "On your left you'll find the Sub-Zero refrigerator that keeps the takeout food fresh."

"Does anybody ever cook?" I ask.

"I don't think so. Melanie brings in a chef every now and then if she's having lots of people over. Otherwise, somebody from Organic Express drops stuff off."

She leads me out of the kitchen and down a short hall lined with Audubon prints, then into a room full of books. The desk probably had to be lowered in with a crane since it's way too big for the door.

"Stay behind the velvet rope, sweetheart."

I know she's just playing docent, but what if she actually liked me? What then?

She points to the desk. "Where Megan's father sat and talked to his bimbo girlfriends."

"So you knew him."

"Oh, yeah. A total sleaze. Put the make on me when I was fourteen. You know how people have stuff and you wish you had it, and then you see what it does to them and you think, 'No, thanks'?"

"You mean money?"

"More like how good-looking he was. Totally gorgeous. But he's just like a prince in one of those stories where some crone comes into the queen's bedroom with a curse up her sleeve. When he grows up, women throw themselves at him, he can't say no, and he can never be happy. He still calls Megan's mom and cries."

I walk to the nearest wall and check out the books. They're real, but they're also stiff. The spines crack when I try to open them.

"Where'd the money come from?" I ask.

"She brought some with her, and he made the rest in real estate."

I run one hand across the amazingly shiny desk. "So," I say, "it's a study, but nobody actually studies in here."

"Megan sometimes. Two years ago she published this essay called 'My Body Is a Treasure I Want to Squander.'

It's already in a couple of anthologies. I know she wrote that here because she told me."

She links her arm through mine and tugs. I try and act like this happens to me all the time.

Just then, we hear a dog bark. "I thought you took care of that," says Wanda.

"It's not him—that's a spaniel."

"So you know all this about animals, just from working in that pet shop of your parents?"

"Mostly. But let's not forget the noble institution of Scouting."

"Seriously?"

"God no. My scoutmaster gave me the creeps."

Wanda grins. "Was he just a total mo?"

"That would've been okay with my dad as long as Mr. Mathis brought all his gay friends in the store to buy teacup terriers."

"He actually said that?"

"Maybe not exactly, but according to him, every black guy's a crack addict, every gay guy's got a little fluffy dog, and every Chinese kid can do calculus in his sleep. The whole reason I was a scout in the first place was because he made me. I was supposed to forge all these relationships, right?"

"Let me guess," says Wanda. "So that every time somebody wanted a parrot, he'd think of you?"

That makes us both laugh. "The whole thing was truly stupid. If all that bogus networking wasn't bad enough, there were badges for everything: Rabbit Raising, Pulp and Paper. There was even something called the American Heritage badge."

Wanda slouches against the wall. If I put one hand next to her and leaned in, I'd be flirting.

"What's an American Heritage badge look like?" she asks.

"Like the Statue of Liberty is holding a ham."

Wanda takes me by the arm again and we set out. She says, "You're kind of cute, you know that?"

I doubt it, but I know for sure I smell good. I took two showers.

Megan's mother's bedroom is huge: his-and-her bathrooms, a spa in one corner, a mini-gym in the other. And a bed that only needs chalk lines to double as a soccer field.

"Watch this," Wanda says, reaching for a remote. One remote among many.

At the push of a button, the blinds open onto another patio: koi pond, one teak chaise, ferns and calla lilies, a statue of a Buddha.

"Holy cow."

She nods. "Yeah, I know. You kind of have to wonder what old Siddhartha would think about ending up in a place like this."

This time she takes my hand. I let her, but I'm not kidding myself. She's just a nice person who is probably this way with a lot of people. This is still maybe the best day of my life.

In Megan's room there's a plasma TV and all those mirrors that Wanda mentioned before. On one of them, right at eye-level, where she can see it from her Stair Master, is a note in Magic Marker: GET THAT BIG ASS OF YOURS UP THOSE STEPS.

Wanda tells me, "Nice, huh?"

"Not so much, actually."

We're on our way back outdoors when she stops me in the door of the music room. There's the biggest piano I've ever seen.

"Does anybody play that thing?" I ask.

"Megan took lessons when she was little."

"My father would say, 'All that money just so some spoiled brat can play "Twinkle, Twinkle Little Star."'"

Wanda leans against the doorjamb and crosses her arms. "My dad was a carpenter. And he had this bumper sticker inside his toolbox that said, EVERY TIME I HEAR THE

WORD *CULTURE*, I REACH FOR MY PISTOL. Not that he actually had a pistol."

"Do you miss your parents?" I blurt.

"I'm too pissed off to miss them."

"I can't hear their voices anymore, you know? I don't remember what my own parents sounded like."

She puts one hand behind my head, sort of on my neck. I stand very still.

"I don't know where that came from," I tell her. "I'm sorry."

Then she leans in and kisses me on the forehead. "Orphans in the storm," she says.

By the pool, Megan and Astin are still making out except now they're wrapped around each other on one chaise.

"Seriously," says Wanda, looking for a place to put her wedge of cheesecake, "can you two do that somewhere else?"

Megan gets to her feet and tugs at her bikini. Astin gropes for a towel. Then he chases her toward the house.

"Oh, Ted!"

When I turn, Megan is standing in the doorway.

"Ted, rinse all those plates, will you? And stack them. Maria will do the rest in the morning."

Wanda says, "Don't pay any attention to her."

"It's okay."

"No, it's not. She can order me around—we're friends. But you're a guest."

"Really, it's no big deal."

"Well, don't do it now. If I put on a CD, will you dance with me?"

Oh, man. "I'm not very good."

"Who is?" She gets to her feet. "You want a little drink? Her mom's got some two-thousand-year-old brandy."

"Okay, I guess."

While Wanda is inside, I rehearse the box step I taught myself by reading a book. I'm hoping she wants to slow dance because that's all I know how to do.

Sure enough, something lazy and bluesy comes from the outdoor speakers. Wanda walks toward me with a glass in each hand and her arms spread wide, like I'm home at last. I know it doesn't mean much, but it's a good feeling anyway.

I take my drink, pretend to sip it, and watch her take a mouthful and lick her lips.

"Doo-wop," she says linking her hands behind my neck. Mine settle at her waist. Wanda's forehead touches mine, like we're aliens saying hello. She sings under her breath, something about the still of the night.

Luckily I can see my feet and they're still moving. Mostly, though, she just sways. She's totally relaxed. I can smell the liquor on her breath, heavy and rich. I try and remember this in case it never happens again.

When the song ends, she yawns. "Do you think sleep really will knit up the ragged sleeve of care?"

"Probably. Are you sleepy?"

She puts one hand to my cheek. "Just a little."

I lead her toward the chaises. "Go ahead. Take a little nap."

"Will you sleep too?"

"Absolutely."

"If I snore, poke me."

"All right."

She reaches across the three or four inches that separate us. "Hold my hand, Teddy."

A hummingbird fools around in the bougainvillea. On the other side of the wall, a car or two goes by. Wanda's breath evens out. Her mouth opens a little.

I remember what Astin said: "It's just a day at the pool with a couple of girls."

How cool is that?

I watch her sleep for a while, then wander into the house to use the bathroom. To get there I have to pass the study. There's that big, shiny desk. I remember the one I ruined at the party in grade school. I swear to God, if there'd been one girl there half as nice as Wanda, that would've never happened.

A little later, when Wanda wakes up, I'm right beside her with my eyes closed. She stirs, and I look over.

"Did I snore?" she asks.

"The earth trembled."

"Shut up!" She runs both hands through her curly hair. "Are those two still inside?"

"As far as I know."

"That just makes me tired. You want a ride home?"

"Sure, I guess."

"It's not a problem. I just live about six blocks from the Rafters, over on Elm."

Outside, we walk down the driveway and head for an old Toyota pickup.

"Megan wants me to park on the street so oil doesn't drip on her precious driveway. She says she hates her mother, but she's just like her. She told me once she wanted to burn this house down and live in the rubble. Then we went uptown and I watched her spend eleven hundred dollars on clothes."

I get in and grope for the seat belt. The truck is messy, but orange peels on the floor make it smell tropical.

"Those books in your way?" she asks.

I look down. "I kind of stepped on one."

"Let me have 'em." And without looking, she sticks one arm out the window and tosses them into the truck bed.

Wanda negotiates the wide streets, yawning a little and squinting into the sun.

"I'm not sure that brandy was a good idea," she says. "I've got a killer headache and a lot of work to do."

A few minutes later she pulls up in front of the Rafters'.

"If you ever want to do something," she says, "I'm good to go. It's not a date or anything. It's just, you know, an outing. A movie or a hamburger at Blue's."

"Are you serious?"

"No, I'm a total sadist. This number belongs to Charles Manson." She rips a piece of paper out of the nearest notebook, writes on it, and hands it to me. "Of course I'm serious. Now you be serious and call me."

I don't want to go in yet, so I sit on the porch. I like everything that happened today: Megan's house, the pool, the lunch, dancing with Wanda, watching her sleep—everything.

A few minutes later, Astin roars up, parks the bike, covers it and tucks it in, then hustles my way.

"How'd it go with Wanda?"

"Great. She's nice."

"Did you make out?"

"We danced and then she said for me to call her."

He pats his leather jacket until he finds his phone, then hands it to me. "So call her."

"She didn't mean now. I just saw her."

"When did she mean?"

"I don't know. Probably somewhere between two and five days. I saw this movie, and one day means you're desperate but anything over five means you're not into her at all."

"Screw the movies. What do they know— they're make-believe. Call her now. She'll love it."

"Are you sure?"

He watches me read off the lined notebook paper, then punch in numbers. I lick my lips while her phone rings.

"Wanda? Hi, it's Teddy."

"Teddy? What's wrong?"

"Uh, nothing. You said to call, so I'm calling."

Then there's an ominous silence. Finally she says, "Are you nuts? I just saw you, and now I'm right in the middle of something. I'll talk to you later."

I hand the phone back to Astin. "She hung up on me."

"Don't sweat it."

"Hey, she was fun today. Now I can't call her back ever. I feel stupid."

"What exactly did she say? Word for word."

"Word for word she said, 'Are you nuts? I just saw you, and I'm right in the middle of something. I'll talk to you later.'"

He leans back and grins. "There you go. Talk to her later."

"No." I shake my head. "Now she's mad. I shouldn't have called her so soon. I shouldn't have listened to you."

"Oh, bullshit. If I did anything, I made you more interesting."

And he was right. Not that I was so interesting, but Wanda looked for me at school the next day and I called her that night.

Pretty soon we're talking a lot—me outside on the

porch with the Rafters' phone and her in bed just before she goes to sleep.

It's just ordinary stuff: what happened at school, my new haircut, how Megan was mad at Astin. Sometimes I hear the Rafters arguing in the kitchen, just like my parents used to.

But there's no reason for me to get a stomachache. They aren't my parents; they're my foster parents. And I've got somebody to talk to.

CHAPTER 8

It's not even a week until Astin graduates and he can't sit still: motorcycle runs up Angeles Crest, over to Blue's, even down to the beach, which he doesn't even like. Sometimes he takes me, every now and then C.W., but mostly Megan.

Tonight we're under the awning just outside Borders books on Colorado Boulevard. All the motorcycles are lined up side by side at the curb: Astin's chopper; a couple of classic Indians; two or three big Yamahas; Noah's bar hopper, which is so cherry he only rides it at night in warm weather; and Warren's Ducati. I dial my new mobile phone.

"Wanda? It's me."

"Teddy! Where are you?"

"Uptown with Astin."

"Are you wearing your leather jacket?"

"Yeah."

"Can you tell yourself from the other guys, or do you get confused?"

"I'm the one drinking the frappe."

Wanda laughs. I really like to make her laugh. She says, "One CPA, one college dropout, a children's book illustrator, a guy who hangs drywall, a transit cop, and a funeral director. Six divorces, a felony for possession, severe liver damage, a heart attack waiting to happen, and about a dozen bad kidneys. What do you see in that scooter trash, anyway?"

"They're Astin's friends; I just keep him company."

"And then there's that. Are you two registered at the Harley- Davidson store yet? It's an all-chrome wedding, isn't it?"

"You are so funny."

"Has Scotty said his bike can blow the doors off anything on the road?"

"Only about six times."

"Do you want me to come get you again?"

"Uh-huh."

"Give me forty-five minutes."

"Why so long?"

"Those guys think I'm just a dumb Betty, but I'm not going to be a dumb Betty who smells like turpentine. I'll take a shower and put on a tank top; that'll start their hearts."

I fold up my little phone and look for someplace to sit down. The only empty chair is at the card table, where three guys I don't know very well are playing Texas Hold 'Em. We're not really supposed to gamble, so there's no money showing; we just remember our bets. I lose a couple of bucks to a guy with a dagger tattooed on his neck, then take a ten-dollar pot when the river card gives me a straight.

Thanks to Astin, I know what to do next. "I'm buying." Actually, thanks to Astin I know what a straight is.

The café is inside the bookstore. I've been here with Astin two or three times now, and I always see somebody from my old high school. They're hanging out or buying a book or just cruising the boulevard. I totally avoid them. I get in another line or pretend to read a book until they're gone. I don't even want to think about that old stuff.

I carry the little cardboard tray outside and hand out the coffees to Matt, Terry, and Sid. I like the way shoppers give these guys their space. Somebody's always got his boots sticking out farther than he should, but nobody ever says anything. They just take a little detour on their way to Urban Outfitters or Restoration Hardware.

Then I sit down by Russ, who carries a fancy chess set in his saddlebags and plays speed chess with anybody who's got ten dollars. But not tonight.

"Hey, Teddy."

"Hey, Russ. Why aren't you playing? You're usually up about fifty bucks by now."

He's wearing a bandanna covered with little skulls. He tugs at it before he says, "I'm bummed. My grandma died, and I got to go back to St. Louis and take care of stuff. There's just me, right? So I gotta find a funeral home and pick out a casket and do all that morbid shit." He sits up straighter. "Everybody says, 'Oh, what a pain in the ass,' but it's not. She was a cool old lady. I lived with her until I went in the service. Without her, man, I'm in jail, you know? She wasn't all churchy or anything. She was just solid. Standin' at the stove when I came home, new notebooks for school, gave a shit if I was late, the whole nine yards."

"My folks haven't been gone all that long."

"Yeah, I remember Astin saying something."

"If I'm out of line here, just tell me, okay?" I scoot my

chair a little closer. "When I had to do what you're going to, I just stood there in front of this wall of caskets and listened to some guy in a suit try and sell me something that'd keep my parents dry forever.

"But I get through that. And I find a minister and he picks a day, and I'm just like walking in my sleep the whole time." I look over at him. I ask, "You okay with this?" But I know he is. He's leaning in.

"Absolutely, man. Keep talkin'."

"So it's finally Saturday and the service is at ten, but I'm there two hours early because the zoo isn't open. I'm walking around, right? Trying not to think too much, and I kind of get toward the back of the place and I can hear these two guys talking behind a door and one of them says, 'I'm not kidding. Twenty-four miles to the gallon.' And all of a sudden I was okay. Or at least a whole lot better."

Russ shakes his head. "I don't get it."

"They were just doing their job, see? My parents weren't my parents to those funeral guys. They were just things to work on. So your grandma is fine. I mean, she's probably in heaven or someplace nice. All you're going to see is her body. All you have to do is take care of business. You can do that."

"Teddy!"

I look over at Astin. I nod and stand up. Russ reaches across the table, puts his arms around me, and pounds on me hard.

"Thanks, man. I mean it."

I make my way over to Astin, who grabs my arm and pulls me into an empty chair. "See that girl in the three-hundred-dollar jeans, the one with the bulldog?"

I look down the block. "Yeah."

"She wants to talk to me. Next time she comes by, call that dog, okay?"

"Will you relax."

"What's up with Russ?"

"His grandma died."

"I thought he didn't like you."

"I didn't know that."

"Yeah, he thinks you're a poser because you don't have your own bike. But a minute ago he was all over you."

"I just gave him some advice."

He nudges me. "Here she comes. Oh, man, she is haughty all over."

"Aren't you going by Megan's in about twenty minutes?"

"I just want to talk to her."

So I say to the dog, "Hey, come over here, okay?"

Bulldogs really do resemble Winston Churchill. This one just looks at me like he's about to address the nation.

I say, "Please. My friend here wants to talk to your owner."

He drags her a step or two in my direction, and that's enough for Astin to start laying out his charms like things at a yard sale.

I put out one hand, but the dog doesn't move. "Are you okay?" I ask. "Does she treat you all right?"

"So you're...one."

"I'm one what?"

"One we...an tlk to."

"You're breaking up on me here. It's like we're on cheap mobile phones." His eyes get a little brighter. He comes closer, close enough to put his paws on my knees. I reach out and rub at the loose skin around his neck. I say, "What's going on, anyway?"

"Teddy," he says, "what...ou...xpect. You're running with...other pack now." Then he drops onto all fours and walks away.

Another pack?

Just then, Wanda pulls up in front of the bookstore, puts her flashers on, gets out, and walks around to the passenger side. She's wearing cutoffs and a red tank top.

"Wanda!" somebody yells. "Dump this kid and ride with me. I need somebody to keep my back warm."

She shakes her head. "You're too old, Scotty. I like 'em very, very young."

Astin hails me. "Cover for me with the Rafters, okay? I might never come home."

I get behind the wheel. Wanda's truck is a lot cleaner because I've been washing it lately. "Thanks for coming up."

"I was tired of packing, anyway. Not that there's all that much. I just talked to my mom on the phone. She's a little mad that the house is going to be empty." She shakes her head. "I'm not having kids." She glances over at me. "Do you want kids ever?"

"God, I don't know."

One hand comes across and rubs my neck. "You okay, Teddy?"

"I guess. I was talking to this guy a few minutes ago and his grandma just passed away, and that made me think of my folks, and then this girl came by with her bulldog, and my mom loved bulldogs, so . . . you know."

"Do you just want to go home?"

"I think so. Is that okay?"

"Sure. We'll do something tomorrow night. I should study, anyway. I've got one more test, the last one I'll ever take in my life. How weird is that?"

That thing about my parents isn't the real reason I don't feel like doing anything tonight. The real reason is I could barely hear that bulldog. The only thing that came through loud and clear was that I'm running with another pack. How can I explain that to Wanda when I don't know what it means myself?

When we get to the Rafters', C.W. is on the porch talking to Barbara and Bob. Standing beside him is a real mutt—wiry-haired, skinny, and seriously in need of a bath.

Wanda parks the truck and we walk up together. We can hear Barbara from the sidewalk,

"It's a dog, Bob. Not a baby. Nobody wants you to adopt a baby. And it won't cost you a penny, so don't worry about your precious certificates of deposit."

C.W. says, "I'll do everything—feed him, wash him, pick up after him. All you got to say is he can stay in the backyard. He'll be a great watchdog, espe cially when Barbara's all by herself."

I glance down at the mutt and try to picture him going for some felon's jugular. I say to him, "Can you hear me at all?"

He just pants a little and leans against C.W.

Barbara says, "He needs a bath."

Wanda says, "He is kind of cute."

C.W. appeals to me. "We can give him a bath, can't we, Teddy?"

"If there's anything I know how to do, it's give a dog a bath."

Mr. Rafter looks like one of those guys on Mount Rushmore.

"Why don't you take the dog for a walk or something," says Barbara. "I've got a few things to say to Bob in private."

"Sure," C.W. says. "Absolutely. Just remember: nothing out of pocket for you guys. I'll take care of that. All I need is a backyard for him to live in."

As we go down the walk toward the street, I say, "He needs a leash."

C.W. shakes his head. "You don't need no leash, do you, boy? You'll stay right beside me."

And he does. I know that he's just scared; his tail is down and kind of tucked under his belly. He probably won't run away.

Wanda puts one arm around me, kisses my cheek, then does the same to C.W. "I'm going to leave you two to deal with this. Call me before you go to sleep, Teddy, okay?"

We watch until she drives away.

"She's nice," C.W. says.

"Yeah."

"But you guys don't do nothin'."

"Not like you mean."

"'Cause she's goin' away and all."

"Sure." But I don't exactly know why we don't. We just don't. And I'm okay with that.

We walk up Wayne Street, past the same houses I saw that first day from Ms. Ervin's van. Except now I know who lives in them. Mr. and Mrs. Spires, Mr. Patterson, Wyatt and Maggie Nelson, Ellen Watson and her little boy, Forrest.

The Rafters wonder how people like Wyatt and Maggie, and Ellen, too, I guess, can afford to buy with real estate prices the way they are. I just guess they saved up or it's worth it to scrimp and cut some corners to live on a pretty street with real trees that've been here forever.

I tell C.W., "Dogs aren't cheap. He needs shots, and if he's not fixed, he needs to get fixed, and he's already big enough to eat like two dollars' worth of food a day."

"I don't care, man. I'll get a job. Listen to this—I'm playin' ball by myself and he just trots up, okay? Watches me shoot. One bangs off the rim and he goes and like gets it. Pushes it with his nose and shit. Almost brings it back to me. What am I supposed to do after all that, leave him there?"

I say to the dog, "You picked yourself a good one, didn't you?"

Nothing. He glances at me, but he takes C.W.'s hand in his mouth and tugs on it.

"Do you believe that, Teddy? He loves me. What kind do you think he is?"

"Just a mix, but that's good. He's for sure not overbred."

"No way Bob says no, does he?"

I shake my head. "I've seen this a hundred times. He's going to be all hard-nosed about him. Lots of rules and what the dog can't do and when he can't do it. Then in about three weeks he'll go to PetSmart and buy him a two-hundred-dollar bed so he can sleep in the same room with him and Barbara. And she'll want to take him whenever she goes anywhere because he's so cute with his head out the car window. No, my friend, your problem is not can he stay. Your problem is going to be visitation rights."

We're walking back when Mr. and Mrs. Spires (he's a physicist and she's married to a physicist, if you get my meaning) stop us. They've got their granddaughter, Kim, in one of those pricey carriages, and the dog puts his paws on the side and looks in.

Mrs. Spires laughs. "What a charming animal," she says. "What's his name?"

I say to the dog, "This is your last chance. Tell me, or who knows what it'll be."

He just leans into C.W.

When I get in bed that night, I'm totally alone. Totally. The lions are gone, the giraffe is gone, and C.W.'s dog won't talk to me. The dark seems darker, the noises louder. Then I remember how Russ told me about his grandmother. How Wanda came and got me, Astin paid for my coffee, and C.W. asked for advice about the pooch.

Is this the new pack I'm running with?

No way am I going to sleep with all that bouncing around in my head, so I just get up and start working out. Which is something I've been doing for a few weeks now. Not much weight, lots of repetitions. I do what Astin says, which is to concentrate on the muscle that's working, because that fills up my mind.

I don't look all that different. Well, maybe I do. A little, anyway. I only check when I'm by myself.

I'm right in the middle of my third set of twenty-five when I hear Astin on the stairs. *Clomp, clomp, clomp.* And then—*boom!* He's right in the room. Tripping over one of the dumbbells. His dumbbells.

"Goddamn it, Teddy."

I carry the weights back where they belong, even

though I know it's too late. "I thought you weren't coming home."

"What the fuck is my stuff doing all over the floor?"

"I'm working out. I was going to put everything away at the same time."

"I told you not to mess around with my stuff."

"You said to ask. And I asked you a long time ago. And you said okay."

"Put this shit away now and keep your goddamn hands off of it, okay?"

"Sure, fine. If you'd give me the sixty dollars you owe me, I could buy some weights of my own."

For some reason Astin zips up his jacket. I don't know why, but it makes me feel cold all over. I put on my pants and tuck my mobile phone in one pocket while he asks, "What fucking sixty dollars?"

I can't back down now. "The sixty I loaned you that day we went over to Megan's."

He digs in his jeans, fumbles with a wad of bills, counts some out, and shoves them at me. "Here, now shut up."

I look at them. "This is thirty-five."

He gets hold of my T-shirt and pulls me right into him. "Will you stop busting my balls?"

I try to get a finger or two between my shirt and my neck, but I can't. "Cut it out. That hurts."

All he does is say it back all high and whiny: "'Cut it out. That hurts.' You little weenie."

"Don't call me names. I hate it when people call me names."

"Oh, yeah? What are you gonna do about it?"

That's when I hit him. And it's a pretty good shot, because I hear him grunt, but the next thing I know, I'm looking at my hand, which I've just had to my nose, and there's blood all over. It takes a few seconds for my face to start to hurt.

"Now get out of here," he says.

"Go to hell. It's my room, too."

He grabs me by the scruff of the neck, walks me to the door, and shoves. A few seconds later the door opens again and my sneaks fly out.

When I get up, I look at myself in the bathroom mirror. My nose and my lip are bleeding, but some cold water and a lot of toilet paper stop that.

Downstairs, Bob is watching TV. He doesn't even look up when I tell him I'm going out, he just grunts. Barbara and C.W. are still on the back porch with Tupac, the dog. I slip out the front door and start walking. All the people I know on the street are in bed or getting ready for bed. There's a light on every so often where maybe somebody is reading or taking an Alka-Seltzer. Not everybody is young or still has a partner. Mrs. Morgan is by herself, and so is Mr. Finch.

The closer I get to Wanda's, the fewer people I know or even know about. It feels chillier. I'm the only one out, so I'm glad when I see Wanda's light on.

I knock but I say, "Wanda! It's me." So she won't get scared.

When she opens the door, she's got a book in one hand and a pencil between her teeth.

"Teddy? What's wrong?"

"I got into it with Astin." I point to my face.

She opens the door wider, and I step inside. She says, "I just got off the phone with Megan. They broke up."

"So that's it."

"Yeah, get used to it. They like to break up. Then they get back together and say, 'Oh, baby, I'm so sorry. It was all my fault.' 'No, no, sweetheart, it was my fault.' And I think you know what happens after that." She points to the couch. "Sit down. I'm either going to finish *Leaves of Grass* or get the lawn mower and run over it."

The couch has flat cushions with corners and spindly legs with brass tips. Her TV is on, and a black woman is crying while a white woman in a spangly dress tells her everything will be all right.

"What are you watching?"

Wanda yells from the kitchen, "That's *Imitation of Life,* the original. Claudette Colbert and Louise Beavers. Louise Beavers's daughter, Peola, wants to pass for white and Claudette Colbert's daughter wants her mom's boyfriend."

"Jeez. And I thought I had problems."

"What's cool is in the middle of all that, Claudette Colbert changes clothes about every ten minutes. The costumes are great. I'm almost done here. Get some ice out of the fridge and hold it against your lip. It'll keep the swelling down."

I do what she says, then wander back to the nearest bathroom and look at myself. I could even have a black eye. How cool would that be?

I've been at Wanda's before, but not for long. Usually she picks me up and we do something like go to the movies, where all she looks at is the sets. Walking out, she always wants to know who shot who and what were all those zombies doing in the mall?

I pick up the remote. "Can I change the channel?"

"Absolutely. It's not like I don't know how it turns out."

Oh, man. There's *7th Heaven,* the show my media

teacher made us watch, the show he called *Just Ask Dad.* Then *Friends,* a kind of super-deluxe foster care without the Rafters. And on AMC an old Tarzan movie. I remember being six years old and wanting to go to the zoo so I could see Simba and Tantor. I didn't want a little brother, either. I wanted Cheetah.

"You all better?" Wanda asks when I go back in the kitchen.

"Yeah. I like knowing it's not me Astin's really mad at, but I'm not sorry I hit him."

She closes her book with a thump. "Last poem I'll ever read in my life, slugger. Let's make popcorn."

She wants nothing to do with hot-air poppers, so there's oil to measure out and a big, clumsy thing to shake over the stove. I start to think about only talking to Wanda on the phone when she's in New York.

Once we settle on the couch, I leave the movie on but hit MUTE. "I saw those boxes with that East Coast zip code."

"Yeah. Tomorrow they go to an address I've never been to where a girl I've never seen will store them in my half of the bedroom. Oh, man, this could be such a big mistake."

I put one arm around her, and all her curly hair makes me have to close my eyes. "It'll be fine."

"God, I hope so. It's just so much like starting over."

"I did that. Sort of. You sure can. You've got a job and everything."

She sighs. "I know." She grabs the cold washcloth and dabs at my lip.

I sit up so I can see her. "Do you know what's weird? These guys in my old high school used to pick on me, but I never hit them back. So then I meet Astin, who turns out to be a pretty good guy, and I end up punching him."

"Guys are always punching each other." She points to the screen. "Look at this. You can always tell the bad natives because they've got bones in their noses, and the good natives always hide the baby elephant."

While I watch the inevitable stampede, I can't help but think about all those animals I used to talk to. Did that really happen?

Wanda turns off the TV, stands up, and yawns. "Do you want to stay here tonight? Sleep in my parents' room? Astin will be on the phone with Megan, anyway."

"Sure, okay."

"Do you want pajamas or anything? My dad wore pajamas, or at least he got them for Christmas every year."

"No, I just... you know. Take off my jeans."

"Yeah, me too."

We walk down the hall together. Wanda's room is first.

I can see her poster of *Barbarella* on the west wall.

"I like it," she says, "that you're not all over me. I like how uncomplicated this is."

"I didn't plan it or anything."

"That's another thing I like." She gives me a sisterly kiss and closes the door.

I wander around her parents' room. There's some kind of grit on the floor, maybe sand. Most of the dresser drawers are standing open; there are two or three hangers on the floor of the closet and a pair of those rubber flip-flops with the rubber daisies.

The bed smells funny. Not bad, exactly, but like somebody else. When I lie down, I slide toward the center.

I touch my lip, which is really starting to throb, find my phone, and dial.

Wanda sounds a little groggy when she answers.

I ask, "How fast did your parents get out of here, anyway?"

"Ted?"

I can hear her tussle with the sheet, and I wonder if she's sitting up.

"They floated a loan," she says, "the day after they knew they won, and that was that."

"There's like a trough in this mattress."

"You're on my dad's side. Switch around."

"I am switched around, but I slide down anyway."

"Why are we talking on the phone, Teddy?"

"We talk on the phone all the time."

"But that's when you're at the Rafters' and I'm here."

I look around the room again. There are two or three dark rectangles on the wallpaper. Where do you hang pictures in a motor home?

"Do you ever come in here?" I ask.

"God, no. It's probably haunted."

"This place makes me think about packing stuff. Did you have to help your parents?"

"A little."

"I had to pack everything. Is there anything worse than your mother's underwear? I mean even Goodwill didn't want it, and there it just was."

She says, "After my folks disappeared into the sunset, I trashed things. I was so mad that sometimes I'd just go find something I thought they might like or that they'd want when they came back, and I'd throw it away. But I promised myself that the minute I got to New York, I'd stop being pissed off."

I switch the phone to my other ear. "I don't know what I am anymore."

"Do you think about your folks every day?"

"Yeah."

"Me too. Do you dream about them?"

"Sometimes."

"It's always me hitchhiking and they just blow right by in that Winnebago or they throw things at me."

"In mine their car's on fire, and my legs weigh about a ton."

We don't say anything for a while, but we know each other is there. A car goes by outside, and those long bars of light slide across the wall and bend when they hit the ceiling.

"Teddy, if I let you come in here, it's just to sleep, okay?"

I get right to my feet. "Sure."

"I'll just never get any rest thinking of you trying to crawl out of that dent in the bed my fat-assed father made."

"I'll sleep on top of the covers. You won't even know I'm there."

"We can't do anything because I'm going away, right?"

"I know."

"But you should want to. You should want to a lot. I should be almost irresistible."

I tell her, "You're totally irresistible."

"And the only reason you don't just ravish me is because you're sweet and considerate."

This kind of reminds me of doing the dozens with C.W. except that it's more true, and it's an easy way to talk about something that's hard to talk about.

I tell her, "I don't want to be sweet and considerate, though. I want to climb up some vines onto your balcony and jump right into your bed."

"It'll be torture for you lying beside me tonight, right? You won't sleep a wink."

"I'll never sleep again."

"Okay, then. You can come over."

When I get next door in my underwear, she has the covers pulled up to her chin and she's grinning.

"Skinny legs," she says. "I love guys with skinny legs."

I unfold the quilt at the end of her bed, lie down, and pull it over me.

"Closer," she says.

I scoot over until I bump into her. It's such an amazing feeling.

"You know what I was just thinking?"

"Uh-uh."

"That the last thing my mother said to me after they won that money was, 'Wanda, you only live once.' And then she put on her sunglasses and got in the motor home."

"The last thing my mother said to me was, 'Feed the cats.'"

I feel her turn away, grope for a Kleenex, and blow her nose. "Put your arm around me, okay?" she asks. "I'm cold."

When the phone rings, Wanda rolls over. "God," she mumbles, "who's that?'

I grope for my mobile.

"Ted, get over here before Bob wakes up."

"Astin?"

"You know what? Never mind. Just meet me outside in five minutes."

"You know where I am?"

"Are you kidding? Where else would you go?"

I hit the red button. I say, "I better get out of here. I'm not supposed to be out all night."

Wanda stretches. She's under the sheet; I'm not. I look around for my pants. "Did you sleep?" she asks.

"Will you get mad if I say yes?"

"Very funny. Do you want anything? I've got milk and cereal and bread and all that stuff."

I find one shoe. "No, I'm fine." I already think I can hear Astin's bike.

She props herself up on both elbows. "Call me, okay? I didn't mean to get you in trouble."

"I'll be all right if Bob's not up and around." I lean in and kiss her on the forehead. She pulls at the covers and turns over.

It's early and it's Sunday. A little kid is the only other person awake, and he's sitting on his porch waiting for the day to start. I remember doing that—roaming the house, looking in cupboards, stepping over animals, sneaking into my parents' bedroom to watch them sleep. I didn't hate them or love them. I just wanted them to wake up.

A minute or so later, Astin comes rumbling up. I take my helmet off the sissy bar, then climb on behind him. We're in the middle of a wide turn when he says, "Sorry about last night. I was out of line. Megan drives me crazy sometimes."

"Just tell me next time, okay?"

"Teddy, you hit me first. My side still hurts."

I lean forward so he'll hear me for sure. "Good."

He's going awful fast for just six blocks, but I still don't hold on to his jacket.

"Your lip okay? Did Wanda kiss it and make it better?"

"Like I'd tell you." And I slap the side of his helmet hard.

"You want me to hit you again? Just keep that shit up."

We're home in two minutes. I help Astin put the tarp over the Harley, and we go in the back door. Tupac, who's lying at C.W.'s feet, doesn't bother to bark.

"Ever vigilant."

"He knows you, Teddy."

Barbara's at the sink, her long hair in a braid hanging outside her pink robe. "Where have you two been?" she asks.

Astin and I look at each other.

"Out," he says. "I'm teaching Teddy how to handle a chopper."

"Well, this is the last piece of bread," she says. "If you want toast, you're going to have to go back to the store."

C.W. starts to give the dog a potato chip and Barbara says, "Outside with that animal!"

"If we go now," Astin says, "can we take the Saturn this afternoon? I need to get stuff for my party. You only graduate once."

Barbara drops the rest of her toast in the garbage. "Do you have twenty dollars? It might need gas."

* * *

Astin wants to price steaks at Bristol Farms, and C.W. thinks we ought to have real, honest-to-God party hats and a banner. But first we stop at the ARCO station on Orange Grove.

Astin leans in and asks, "Got twenty bucks, Teddy? I'll pay you right back.

"Oh, bite me."

He starts pumping gas, and I ask, "You guys want something to drink?"

I don't have to say that twice. I walk in, score three cans and some jerky for Tupac, and start back toward the car. I'm wearing a sport coat that Wanda and I found on sale, and I like the way the Coke cans make the pockets sag. It's when I stop looking at myself in the big glass door that I see him—Scott McIntyre. Sitting in his Mustang, which I'm glad to see looks a little worse for wear.

He's got his check register propped on the steering wheel, and he's frowning at it. If he sees me and if he gets out and starts something, we'll take care of him. Astin, C.W., and me. Me first, though.

It's a big station with a dozen of those pump islands. It'd be easy to just walk around him. Tack windward and eventually heave to. Take the low road. Slink away.

I walk right toward him. I come at him from the front. I stop by the open window. I say, "Hey, Scott."

He looks up. "Hey, man." He points to his checkbook. "Where's the money go, huh?"

"No kidding." I watch him add, then say, "Well, see you."

"Yeah."

It's either my new clothes or my new haircut, or he just doesn't care anymore.

I'm almost to the car when C.W. points out the window. "Look, Tupie, it's Ted. Oh, my God. What's that in his hand? Is it a treat? Is it a treat for the best dog in the world? I bet it is."

I climb in, break the jerky in pieces, and start feeding Tupac. Astin knocks on the window. "Don't get Coke all over that upholstery!"

Then he drops the squeegee, grabs his receipt, and gets in. I hand him the cold, wet can as McIntyre's Mustang pulls out. Astin points. "Who's that, anyway?"

"Remember the football player I told you about, the one who wouldn't leave me alone? That was him."

"Scott McIntyre, the quarterback? Really? Let's follow him, and when he gets out of the car, we'll kick his ass."

"He's just going to Kinko's."

"How do you know that?"

I point to my chest. "He's got this stupid name tag on. He's just a stupid guy with a stupid name tag."

"I could still hold him while you hit him."

I reach for my seat belt. "Nah, I'd rather go buy stuff for your party."

CHAPTER 9

Los Angeles is great in the summer. Warm—okay, hot sometimes—but cool at night, even in my attic. Which I've got to myself now, and Barbara bought me a fan to replace the one Astin stole.

I love my job at the zoo. It's just twenty minutes on the Gold Line to Union Station, then fifteen more on a DASH bus. At six in the morning, the guys I work with and I are just about the only ones dashing anywhere. We're for sure the last to get off at the end of the line. Rodney's always wired on coffee and talking to his girlfriend; Jesse sleeps the whole time; Will and I talk about animals because he's nearly as into them as I am. I rethink my future about every ten minutes. One day it's lions and tigers; the next it's sled dogs in Alaska. They've even got an internship right here for grad students in zoology. But basically, I just don't know.

I like walking in through the EMPLOYEES ONLY door. I even like the locker room, which is totally different from the one at high school. Nobody's snapping towels at me, for one thing. Nobody's calling me names. The other guys talk about a movie they've seen or some girl they got to flirt with up by the reptile house. They plan things and ask if I feel like going along.

Then it's time to go to work. The zoo is really at its best in the morning. The animals seem more like themselves. Maybe they don't like being stared at, something I understand. I don't really like seeing them in cages, but I know that's not going to change for a long time, so my job is to make things as good as they can be. They shouldn't be hungry. They shouldn't be sick. Their pens and enclosures should be clean and safe.

I've already graduated from kid-with-a-broom-and-a-burlap-bag to delivery boy. Before we open for business, I like zipping around in my miniature truck with the flatbed that holds boxes of napkins and toilet paper and cases of Snapple one day and bigger boxes of horse meat for the tigers the next.

There's usually a keeper walking around with a chimp or sometimes a python, and always Larry the llama, who was born in the zoo and imprinted on Rusty, his trainer.

Before the day's over, though, I always see somebody who reminds me of my mom or dad, and I wonder what they'd think about what I'm doing. Mom would probably like it, and Dad? Man, who knows? I'm not making a lot of money, that's for sure.

This morning I'm sitting in the truck at the corner of Koala Street and Roo Lane when Larry the llama wanders by a few yards behind Rusty as usual. Larry looks like he always looks, which is a periscope on four legs. Today he stops and stares at me, so I stare back. He nods, so I nod.

"Hey, Teddy."

What the... I thought that was...

Then Sarah tugs at my official khaki shirt. "Didn't mean to scare you," she says.

"No, really, it's okay. I just didn't see you. I was thinking."

She pretends to look mad. "Any more of that, young man, and no dessert."

Sarah is nice; she works the café in the African sector. I give her rides in my little open-air truck all the time.

"Big weekend," she says, climbing in and bracing her

long legs against the dash. "Protests, TV crews, movie stars, the whole nine yards."

"Those guys are right. Somebody should protest. If there's fifty million left in the budget, half of it shouldn't go to advertising the new elephant grassland. It should go for more grassland. People will want to see elephants being pretty much like they would be if they could be."

Sarah nods. She looks kind of sleepy. "Are you working Animals After Dark?"

"For sure. I love Animals After Dark. I get my very own flashlight. What about you?"

"Not this time. I have to look for a new apartment. My roommate used to bring home guys. Now she chants and burns incense."

"My friend Astin is looking."

"He's not living at Megan's anymore?"

I shake my head. "Yeah, but he says her mom is im possible. He's coming today; I got some passes."

Sarah points and I pull into the shade. "Drop me here, okay? I've got to put some potato salad out in the sun for people who get on my nerves. 'Where are the bears?' she says, pretending to be a cranky mom. 'Why aren't the bears out here juggling four or five hoops so I can take their picture?'" She takes her head in both hands. "It's enough to drive a girl crazy." Then she pats my leg and hops out. "Just Astin today?"

"No, Megan for sure. C.W. and maybe Belle."

"Bring 'em by the Serengeti. I'll hook you guys up with some primo tuna salad."

I make my deliveries, then pull on some boots and go to work behind the scenes. Trainers are supposed to clean up where the animals sleep, but usually somebody like me does it instead. It's not too bad, and I like thinking about the antelope or the yak or the wildebeest coming back inside after a day of being stared at and finding everything clean and dry.

Then I wash up and go wait for my friends by the gift shop. Astin will be in his leather jacket, Megan in something short, C.W. in that linen shirt he just bought. The first thing he'll say is that Tupac looked so cute sleeping on my bed, but I shouldn't worry because he'd just had a bath and was almost dry.

I'll tell Megan I talked to Wanda, who says hi, and Megan will say that she'll absolutely call her this time because she misses Wanda like crazy. But she'll forget.

I've got my official khaki shirt on, so people stop and ask me things. A lot of times it's just where the bathrooms are, but other stuff too. And most of the time I know the answers: that baboon's behind is all red because it's

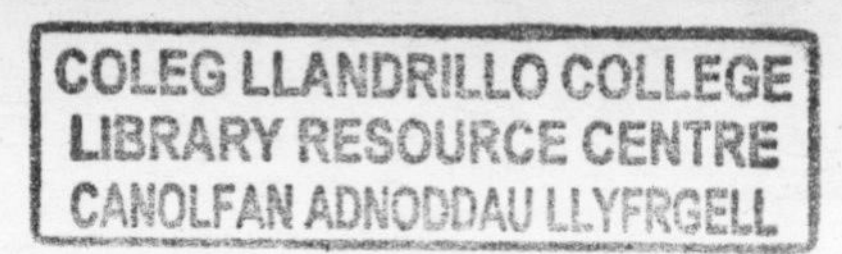

mating season; the old lion's mane is falling out because he's got a fungus that we're treating; the flamingos' wings are clipped because otherwise they'd fly away.

I can kind of picture myself, taller and stronger, wearing scrubs with just a little blood on them because I had to operate on a paw or a hoof or even untangle an intestine.

Then I spot Astin, and I'm sixteen again, making seven-fifty an hour and driv ing a little truck. Oh, well.

Megan sees me and waves, so I step out of the shade. It's time to show my friends around, then buy them some lunch at the Serengeti Café, where Sarah has a handmade RESERVED sign on the best table in the place.